Camp 80

Lee Ducote

GRAVE DISTRACTIONS PUBLICATIONS
NASHVILLE, TENNESSEE

Camp 80

Lee DuCote
Copyright © 2016 Lee DuCote.
Grave Distractions Publications
Nashville, Tennessee

ISBN-13: 9781944066123

In Publication Data
DuCote, Lee
Camp 80
Primary Category: Fiction Themes/Aging
Secondary Category: Fiction Themes / Friendship

Editor – Merrell Knighten
Cover Designer–Marianne Nowicki

Dedicated:

This series is dedicated
to my first love...
my mother.

Also by Lee DuCote

Fields of Alicia

Waterproof

Across Borders

Micah: The Sword of Malachi

Chapter 1

The thoughts emerged slowly... *The retirement community might file bankruptcy?*

Derrick St. Clair, the lead social worker for Cedar Branch Retirement Community, walked slowly through the quad toward the offices, his normal route every morning for the last five years. He gave a reverent smile to a group of men enjoying their coffee while one of them fed the Koi fish with a small handful of crackers.

Be prepared, he recalled the director's instructions. *We might all be looking for jobs.*

Derrick played the conversation over and over in his head; this was a job he had fought to get, and now five years later the thought of hunting for another job sickened him.

Cedar Branch was founded 20 years earlier by an eccentric widow who believed community was the key to living, something that had turned into a proverb and proven itself to be true at the retirement community. CBC, the nickname many of the residences had given it, was divided into three divisions. The Tower and Loft Apartments allowed independent living; the Charleston housed assisted living, and the Health Center was for total care and rehabilitation. Derrick had worked his way up through the assisted living program to the independent living division and then to the position he held now, orientation director.

Walking up to the office, he held the door open for his co-worker. "Good morning," he smiled.

"Is it? I was told to meet the director first thing this morning," Kat replied. Katlyn Rose was on her third year as a social worker and had just begun working alongside Derrick within the last month.

"No worries," Derrick answered, not knowing what to say.

The two of them entered the over-decorated foyer and proceeded down a long hallway leading to the director's office. Oil paintings of nature scenes lined the walls of the hall with a few tables with silk flowers resting in vases on top.

Derrick knocked on the open door with the back of his hand. "You ready to meet with us?" he asked.

A lady behind a dark mahogany desk waved them in. "I hope your day off was good," she said to Kat.

"It was."

"Pull the door closed and have a seat," she said, putting away a set of files.

Derrick shut the door and sat in one of the two leather high-back chairs facing the desk. "I spoke to Derrick about this yesterday," she started. "Because of economic reasons beyond our control, there is a good possibility that Cedar Branch will be forced into bankruptcy. With this, the board doesn't see any way of pulling ahead financially and believe it is best to either sell or close down." The director grimaced.

"Cedar Branch is closing?" Kat asked, shocked at the news.

"That is a strong possibility."

"What will happen to the retirees?" Kat asked.

"Well, it isn't something that would happen overnight. It would take several months and give ample time for everyone to find new lodgings." The director sat back in her chair.

"That's horrible! What about the people that are just now moving in?"

"We can't make changes until the board has made their final decision. I have the highest respect for you and Derrick and wanted you to know well in advance so that if it did happen, you guys would be able to make a change."

"The board doesn't meet again until the 28th of this month. So there are three weeks that will run as normal," Derrick said, assuring Kat.

"Three weeks to not say a word. Am I clear?" the director asked Kat.

"Yes, ma'am."

"But three weeks for you to start looking for another job," she added. Kat sat quietly, trying to absorb the news. She loved her job and since being placed with Derrick on orientation had only grown to love it more. The director picked up her phone. "Is Simon here?" she asked her assistant.

"Yes, he is standing in front of my desk," the female voice replied.

"Send him in." She hung up the phone, adding, "Remember, not a word. This is strictly between us." Derrick and Kat nodded in agreement.

The door swung open with a long-haired mid-20's young man standing in the doorway. "You rang?" he said in a facetious tone.

"Please have a seat." The director pointed to a couch behind the two chairs that Derrick and Kat occupied. "I have asked Simon to make this orientation trip with you guys; the reason is we have six retirees attending, all over the age of 80."

"All over 80?" Derrick asked, receiving a file folder from the director. She handed Kat and Simon one.

"Yes, but all are very active and very well capable of taking care of themselves."

"I appreciate the extra help, but if they are all healthy and of sound mind, why are we taking Simon?" Kat asked, then turned to him on the couch, adding, "No offense."

"None taken," he saluted her.

Cedar Branch's motto was Community starts with relationships, and the independent living division had always offered a one-week trip before moving in. The intent was for the new residents to build a relationship with each other before living in the same community. The orientation week had proven to work and build fellowship.

"Dude, a camp for old people," Simon replied, looking at his file.

Derrick and Kat turned in their chairs and faced the young man. "It is an orientation trip," Kat replied.

"Call it what you want, it's still camp! I'm in," Simon smiled.

Kat turned to the director in search of censure. To her surprise, the director smiled, "Yes, it is camp. But retired people would rather have it called something less juvenile," she instructed.

"But isn't that what old people are looking for, youth?" Simon asked.

Derrick laughed, "I believe you are on to something."

Simon sat up on the couch at being praised. "We could call this week Camp 80!" he joyfully exclaimed.

Kat gave Derrick a dirty look. "It is called an Orientation trip!" she insisted.

"You guys can figure out the terminology on your own. Let's go over the retirees that will be attending this week," the director interrupted, sitting back in her chair.

Chapter 2

In a small, romantic town in southern Alabama, Karl and Betty Rutherfurd were packing the remnants of what was left over from their estate sale. Karl, who was still struggling with the thought of so many people in his house during the sale, had been searching for his autographed baseball for two days. His oldest son was patiently sitting at the table waiting for his father to calm down and take his word that it was packed.

"Dad, please sit. I personally packed your office."

"And you're sure you packed my collection." Karl stopped and faced his son.

"If we don't find it, I'll get you another one."

Karl gave his son a bleak stare. "Mantle has been dead for twenty years."

"I don't mean I'm going to get him to sign a ball, I mean we'll order another from a collector. Don't worry about it, I packed it."

With disbelief, Karl continued digging through the boxes that were still in the house awaiting loading into a moving truck. The Rutherfurds had decided to move to the upscale retirement community after their last close friend passed away from a heart attack. Their oldest son, a successful and wealthy attorney, objected to the move and offered to move them into his guest house. Still, with persuasion from his mother that fellowship was their reason, he gave in and financially supported his parents into a comfortable living.

Betty walked in the kitchen with her ice tea and notepad, two items that she was rarely seen without. "Will you listen to James? He *said* it was packed."

"I'll feel better once I find it," Karl replied with his face buried in a cardboard box.

Betty flipped open her notebook and studied a few pages. "Here! I wrote down that it was packed in a box marked office."

Karl gave her a dirty look. "You know I've been looking for it for two days. You could have told me that earlier," he snapped and walked out flailing his arms.

"I forgot I wrote it down," she replied.

"That's why you carry the notebook—so you won't forget!" he barked back and started searching for the marked box.

"The older he gets, the more dramatic everything is," she commented, looking at her son.

"I'm going to let you guys handle this. Call me if you need me." He kissed his mother on the cheek and left.

Karl and Betty had celebrated their 52nd anniversary eight months earlier, and with their three kids present, surprised them with the news of moving. Karl walked back into the kitchen carrying an old leather book that he carefully placed on the table and opened the cover. The yellow pages crackled, not having been open for years, and the bookmark was still in place where Karl had left off his reading.

"What did you find?" Betty asked, looking over his shoulder as he sat.

"One of my grandfather's astronomy books," he replied, having forgotten about the baseball.

Karl was the grandson of a famous astronomer who helped pioneer the study of stars and planets, placing himself in the history books. Many nights as a young boy, Karl would stay up with his grandfather and watch him document his discoveries, often allowing the young boy to gaze into the heavens through his telescope. Enamored with his grandfather, Karl promised himself he would become an astronomer in his later years, a promise that was broken when a lack of finances prevented sending him to school.

Through several years of working in a bakery, Karl was able to put himself through school in a local college, earning a degree in marketing. It was in the small college that he met Betty, who was finishing her degree in teaching. After a short time dating, the two married, and while Betty taught at the local elementary, Karl was able to finish school.

"I'm going to walk out and check the mail," Betty said, slipping into her sweater.

"Mail doesn't come until 2," he replied, fixated on the old book.

She finished buttoning her sweater, gathered her glass of ice tea, and made her way outside. After a few minutes, Karl began thinking about her outside and followed through the door that had been left opened. Stopping shy of leaving the garage he admired her walking back up the driveway staring into the bright blue sky, unaware of his existence.

"Are we messing up?" he asked her as she got close.

A warm, gentle smile welcomed him. "No, Karl, we're not messing up."

He turned and looked at all the boxes lining the garage, adding, "I don't know. We've worked so for our things, and now we're selling and storing them."

She reached out for his hand. "Come on, let's walk down to the bakery." He looked back at the door that was unlocked, and reading his mind, said "It will be fine." She lured him to the sidewalk.

They strolled slowly down the neighborhood street that quickly opened to the streets of the small, quiet town with local shops and restaurants. Autumn had arrived weeks earlier, and the leaves from the maple trees glowed in bright yellow. The historical old oak trees left leaves covering the ground, creating a canvas of fall, a time of year that both Karl and Betty loved and something else to add to his growing remorse in selling their home.

"I can almost taste the banana nut bread," Betty smiled.

"You're not going to miss this?" Karl continued to doubt.

"Of course I am going to miss this, but I am looking forward to a new chapter in our life and friends, new friends. Plus you know Cedar Branch has a bakery."

"It's not Randy's Bakery," he huffed.

"Remember our promise. If this doesn't work out, then we move back here and live at one of the townhomes." She tugged at his arm while holding hands.

"It's still not Randy's," he answered under his breath.

Betty steered him toward the red brick bakery that poured the aroma of fresh bread into the streets and sidewalks. A younger couple walked by, pushing a stroller while devouring ice cream cones. The young lady smiled at Betty, noticing the sweet gesture of the retired couple holding hands. "There are days I miss raising our children," Betty pointed at the stroller, "but I enjoyed the days and years that followed," she said to the young lady.

"They never grow out of whining," Karl said, looking at the couple.

"Oh, hush, you old fuddy-duddy." She playfully pushed him.

Karl opened the door for Betty, and together they entered the bakery, "Dang nab-it, I forgot what I wanted," she exclaimed.

"You didn't write it down," Karl devilishly grinned.

"I didn't have to—I remember." She walked up to the counter, saying, "I would like a slice of lemon custard pie."

Karl rolled his eyes, asking "What happened to the banana nut bread?"

Chapter 3

A 1975 Oldsmobile sat idling outside the hardware store in Camden Arkansas. Inside buying hardware for a bathroom door were June and Violet Stevens. The Stevens sisters had moved to Camden after receiving an inheritance from a late uncle. The inheritance included a two-story Victorian home, several thousand acres in timber, and the lime green car that waited for them outside. Neither of the women had ever married, and they had lived together their entire life.

"Just get the damn doorknob and let's go." Violet impatiently tapped her foot at the end of the aisle.

"Hold your horses—we gotta make sure it fits," June replied, reading the box.

"It's a door knob! They all fit."

A young man appeared at the opposite end of the aisle from Violet. "Ms. Stevens, you sure you don't need my help?" he asked for the third time.

"No, I believe this will work. It does have a lock, right?"

"Yes ma'am." The young man replied.

"You don't need a lock with the pad lock you installed inside the bathroom." Violet's voice could be heard from the next aisle over.

The young man gave a puzzled look as June flipped her long grey hair over her shoulders and walked toward the cash register. After paying for the door knob, both June and Violet made their way to the car. Jimmy, a high school boy they paid to drive them around town after school, waited behind the wheel.

Violet climbed into the front seat with June seated behind her in the back; putting the car in reverse and slowly backing out, Jimmy slammed on the brakes at Violet's sudden outburst.

"Stop the car!" Violet yelled.

Jimmy's eyes widened as the startling outburst caused his heart to race as if he had just been scared in a haunted house. "What's the matter? Did I hit something?" he asked.

Violet turned in her seat. "You need to scoot to the middle of the back seat. Are you crazy?" she asked June.

"Oh, for goodness' sake, we're just going down the road," June replied, but still moving to the middle of the seat, knowing she wasn't going to win the argument that the car needed to be balanced with riders while going down the street.

"OK, now we can go!" Violet snapped at Jimmy after June moved into place.

Cautiously pulling out onto the street, Jimmy commented, "Ms. Stevens, if you don't mind me saying. These cars are heavy enough that it doesn't matter where people sit—the car is balanced." Jimmy swallowed.

Violet cut her eyes over to the young boy. "Are you in command of this vehicle?" she asked.

Jimmy thought for a moment, not knowing how to answer the question. "Well, I am driving," he cautiously replied.

"Driving doesn't give you command. Home!" She pointed in the direction of their Victorian-style home.

Camden was a small town that thrived in the 70's and 80's from the timber industry and the large paper mill that sat abandoned on the outskirts of town. After the mill closed and over a thousand people lost their jobs, the town was faced with extinction. At one time Camden had over 100 Victorian homes scattered throughout the neighborhoods, but now less than twenty survived. The car slowed while crossing the railroad tracks and turned beside the train depot that was now a local hamburger joint.

Jimmy pulled the Oldsmobile past the short drive that led to their carport and threw his arm on the seat to back up into the dilapidated carport. "Help June with the bags," Violet ordered, opening her door.

"Yes ma'am," Jimmy replied and opened the trunk to get the bags from the grocery store they had visited before the hardware store. Violet walked up the steps and unlocked the side door. "Why does she insist on locking the side door if she wants the front door to remain open?" he asked June.

"You're asking me why my sister is crazy?" June smiled and held her arms out for a couple of bags. "She thinks the neighbors are out to get her," she added, pointing across the street.

"They could just walk around to the front of the house," he said.

June shook her head. "She's just crazy. Say, when are you getting your driver's license?"

"Well, I failed the test again yesterday," Jimmy answered, embarrassed. As he handed her a paper bag, a box of Depends fell out. He reached down for the box and saw it was adult diapers.

"Something to look forward to when you get old," June winked at him and turned to walk in. "We entered the world wearing them, and we'll leave the world wearing them" she shouted as the screen door closed behind her.

"Geez, why can't I get a normal job?" Jimmy whispered to himself, walking up the steps.

After shutting the door with his foot, he set the three bags on the table and started helping June put away the cans of vegetables they had brought. He glanced out the kitchen window to the garden in the back yard. *I spend all summer weeding their garden and they buy their vegetables.* Both sisters were convinced that the local paper mill had contaminated their soil with the leftover pulpwood. *It's wood! How can leftover wood contaminate dirt?* Jimmy asked himself, putting away the canned vegetables.

"Jimmy, take this box to the door down the hallway." Violet handed him an unopened box. "And remember—"

"Don't go in," he interrupted her, knowing that wasn't possible with the eight padlocks that lined the outside of the mysterious door.

A knock sounded from the side door. Violet looked at June. "I bet it's the neighbors," June replied with a devilish grin.

"Get the bat!" Violet's eyes grew wide.

"Relax! It's Mr. Hettsle." June walked over to the door and opened it.

Mr. Hettsle was a local attorney who helped with the sisters' estate and inheritance. He had gained the trust of the quirky old maids after they overheard him talking about saving the soon-to-be-extinct blue-bill duck. Unbeknownst to them, he was reciting a joke, but after receiving his first payment, he decided to keep his secret.

"How's the fight to save the ducks?" June greeted him.

"Still fighting. Not many people interested in saving the poor creatures," he replied, removing his hat as he entered the kitchen.

"You let us know if they need any more money," Violet replied.

"I will. Are you ladies sure about this move?" he asked.

"Yep, you still going to help look after this place?" June asked.

"Yes, I'm still going to help."

Earlier last week, the sisters had sprung the news on him that they were moving to a retirement community. It was a move that nobody saw coming, and many questioned why the crazy sisters would make such a drastic move, but it was amazing how free guitar lessons for residents could lure people in.

Jimmy walked in the kitchen. "If there's nothing else, I better be getting home."

"Thank you, Jimmy," Violet answered, digging in the pantry for a soda.

"You ladies still have that boy drive you around even though he doesn't have a license?" the attorney asked.

"He's gotta learn," June answered, seeing nothing wrong with the situation.

"Well, OK." He started toward the hallway, adding, "I'll be back tomorrow to pick you up and drive you to Cedar Branch. I'll let myself out the front door," he said.

Violet stuck her head out of the pantry. "That would be best—don't want the neighbors thinking any different."

About what? he thought.

"Bye, Mr. Hettsle," June waved.

He tipped his hat and headed out.

"What a nice man," June said.

Walking through the hallway, Mr. Hettsle stopped at the mysterious door and fumbled with one of the padlocks. "Soon as these two crazy old maids are gone, you'll be cut off and what's behind this door will be mine," he said to the lock.

Chapter 4

Sitting on the edge of a queen size bed, a mild and meek gentleman stared at a portrait of a beautiful grey-haired lady. "Doris, I hope this is OK," The man said to the picture. The sound of the front door closing echoed through the empty apartment.

"Dad?" A voice yelled from the kitchen.

"In here," the man replied.

"Are you ready to pack this room? It's the last one," his son replied, walking into the bedroom that showed no signs of anyone moving.

Gerald Harriman had become a widower eight months earlier, and at the age of 84, he thought it would be a good idea to move where he wasn't alone. After taking three months to sell the idea to his son, they ventured out and visited many retirement communities before landing on Cedar Branch. The drive wasn't far from their Atlanta home, and now with his grandkids in college, his son and daughter-in-law would be able to make frequent trips.

He slowly stood from the foot of the bed and placed the framed picture on the window sill. Opening the closet door, he took out the last suitcase resting on the top shelf and set it on the foot of the bed. Opening it, he felt the air leave his lungs, "Oh my!" He gasped.

"What's the matter?" His son looked on concerned.

"Well," he explained. "Here are your mother's shoes that she had been looking for nearly a year." He removed a small but simple pair of gold-laced flats. As he lifted them to eye level, the memories flowed out like water.

Gerald and Doris had decided to cash out a bank CD and invest in a memorable ocean holiday. The week-long cruise boarded in Jacksonville Florida and toured around the panhandle of the sunshine state. The memory was so vivid that Gerald could almost smell the rose-scented perfume that Doris wore along with the glimmering flats. They danced on the Deco Level dance floor to Kenny Rogers's song *Lady*. Once finished, they received a standing ovation, not for their dance skills, but for the depiction of a couple that had been in love for many years.

Years of working in the hotel business had sufficiently prepared them for a comfortable retirement, years that built as many memories. Their son had worked his way through college and grad school in the family business and had now run the successful company for over 20 years.

"Dad, you OK?"

"Yes." Coming out of his trance, he added, "I'll empty the dresser drawers if you will get the things from the shelves."

Together they worked, removing items that had been in place since their move to the apartment. The sound of the door closing came again from the kitchen and two sets of footsteps entered the bedroom. "Hey, grandpa," a young female voice came from the doorway.

"Oh, my goodness," Gerald looked up, finding both of his grandkids in the room.

"We figured that we could miss a few days of class to come see you off," his grandson commented, hugging the small, wiry man.

Gerald's son smiled. "You two are just in time. By the time we finish packing this room, your mom will be back, and the movers should be here anytime." He looked at his watch.

"Well," the granddaughter replied, "where can we start?"

"If I wouldn't have packed everything, we could have tea," Gerald replied.

"We can stop on the way to Cedar Branch—the kids are going with us," his son answered.

A smile formed on the old man's face, and together with his grandkids, they had his bedroom packed in boxes and in the last remaining suitcase with the flats tucked on the bottom. The roar of a heavy truck shook the small apartment as it made its way down the narrow street.

"Sounds like the movers are here," his grandson said.

Looking out the window, Gerald commented, "Hard to believe they could get that truck down the street."

Walking back into the bedroom, his son picked up a box. "Kids, let's get these boxes to the living room, and we will be done."

Gerald watched his family remove the cardboard boxes from his bedroom, leaving only the suitcase and himself. His granddaughter reached down for the plaid suitcase. "I'll get this," he told her. "Give me just a second," he asked.

Replying with only a smile and understanding that he wanted his time, she left him alone. He set the suitcase back on the mattress, placed the portrait of Doris on the top, and zipped it closed. He looked around the bare room and empty walls, feeling a lump in his throat as he fought back the tears. Then, only whispering so his family wouldn't hear him, he said, "I don't know how long I'm supposed to stay here, and I hope you're preparing the way for me." A single tear made it past his shaking hand as he wiped his cheek. "I miss you, Doris."

With a quivering lip and a gentle nod, Gerald walked out of his bedroom for the last time and made it to the living room, where he found three large moving men and his son giving instructions. His grandson put his arm around him, asking "Are you ready for the good life, grandpa?"

Wanting to answer the question differently, he replied, "Yea, I guess so."

They walked to the SUV that was parked next to the curb. Gerald set the suitcase in the back and shut the door, turning around and taking one last look; after another nod, he smiled and climbed in the back seat of his son's vehicle.

Chapter 5

In an upper echelon high-rise in the center of Manhattan, Jack Goslin was giving his personal assistant instructions on packing his belongings when a light knock came from the opened front door.

Jack looked up, saying "Come in," as he waved the assistant building manager to come in.

"Mr. Goslin, I have two tickets to tonight's game. You interested?" he asked.

"You trying to keep me here?" Jack smiled.

"Yes sir, I am."

Jack was a smooth-talking retired real estate agent who had the demeanor of someone that everyone loved, including three of his five ex-wives. He was born and raised on the beaches of south Alabama, but had followed his second wife to the Big Apple 55 years earlier. With only one son, who was as successful in real estate as he was, Jack stayed in New York despite his failed marriages.

"You give them to someone who would appreciate the

game as much as I do," Jack added, putting his hand on the young man's shoulder.

"That's the problem, Jack, nobody appreciates the game more than you."

Giving him a wink, Jack replied, "You'll find someone."

"Mr. Goslin?" His assistant walked back in the room, "Your father's memorabilia is packed. I have marked the boxes for your son to take."

"Thank you; I'm hopeful he'll display it and not pack it somewhere." Jack was the son of an All-American baseball player. During the post-war era, baseball became the American sport, and even though Jack knew his father was a great player, he never got to see him because of all the traveling from game to game. When Jack was 12, his mother had all she could bear of an absentee husband and father and packed his father's things for him to collect on his next time by the house.

"Well," his assistant brushed his slacks off. "I believe that is everything. Shall I walk you down?"

"No, give me a minute, and I'll meet you in the lobby." Jack took a deep breath and walked back through his Manhattan apartment. He had decided in his early 60s that marriage wasn't for him and he would trek through his remaining years alone. His son hadn't spent much time with him because of the business of real estate, making Jack wonder if he had shown his son enough attention growing up. Preparing for the new inhabitants, the marble tile floors had recently been polished, casting the reflection of a tired, elderly man. Jack had been alone long enough and was looking forward to being around people again.

He pulled the door closed and strolled to the elevator

with a spring in his step, something he didn't expect. *Is this happy to be leaving or happy to be arriving*, he thought, pushing the down button that called the elevator.

"Mr. Goslin!" the elevator operator announced as the doors opened. "Is this our last trip?" he asked.

"I'm afraid so," Jack answered.

"You got some last bit of advice for my lady troubles?" the elevator operator asked with a smile, showing his bright and shiny gold tooth.

"Stay away from the ones that will knock your teeth out," Jack answered, looking down as he entered the elevator.

Before pushing the lobby button, the elevator operator replied, "They'll all do that if you make 'em mad." He laughed.

Watching the numbers click by above the door, Jack thought about how many times he had ridden in the elevator—too many times to count. "I'm sure going to miss you, Mr. Goslin, please don't forget to write. Unless you're too busy with a lady," the elevator operator laughed again.

Jack took another deep breath as the doors opened to a lobby full of friends and staff from the building. A smile formed on his face as everyone lined up to the door to take their turn shaking and hugging the well-loved man. Jack turned to the elevator operator and shook his hand with both of his hands, saying, "Take care, my friend."

As Jack was hugging a few of the cleaning ladies, a well-dressed lady in her 50s stepped forward. "I'm going to miss my invites," she said, smiling.

"We can go get that drink now, never too late." Jack motioned to the door.

"Don't stop asking," she hugged him and kissed him on

the cheek.

The last person in line was Bob Stearns, the building manager. He stood at attention with his arm crossed in front of him, revealing the crisp clean sleeves of his Armani suit. "I never thought I'd see the day that Jack Goslin moved to a retirement home."

"Retirement community," Jack corrected him.

"The difference is?" Bob questioned.

"I'll let you know." Jack held out his hand, but Bob reached around him and hugged him tight. Of all the people in New York City, Bob was Jack's closest friend. "I am going to miss you," he told Bob.

"You have your cell phone," Bob hinted to stay in touch.

"If I could learn how to work the damn thing," Jack replied, pulling out a new smart phone from his pocket. Years earlier, Bob was having severe marital problems, and with surprising counseling from Jack, he and his wife worked things out and have been happily married since. Jack reminded him daily that what one cannot do, he must teach; put your wife first in all things and it will work out. That advice Bob received over many glasses of whisky and cigars.

Bob escorted him outside to an awaiting town car and a few other local people saying their goodbyes. "Remember, if south Alabama isn't welcoming you, come back here," Bob reminded him.

"I will." Jack pulled the door closed, saying "To the airport."

Jack turned in his seat and looked back as the town car sped through the busy streets of New York City. The staff stood in one place waving until the car disappeared into a herd of yellow cabs and delivery trucks, Bob standing in front of them at his usual attention with arms crossed in front of his body. Jack spun back around and looked out the windshield, wondering what was next.

Chapter 6

Derrick and Kat sat across from each other at a dark wooden conference table, the files of their retirees attending the week-long trip scattered in front of them. Kat was punching the keys of her laptop finishing the agenda for the week, and looking back at the title, she rolled her eyes: Camp 80. Pressing the *Enter* button on the keyboard, she said, "Ok, it's printing," and closed her laptop.

Simon walked in. "Where do you want them to put their luggage?" he asked.

"I'll be right out. They can leave it in the meeting room for now," Derrick answered.

With a salute, Simon disappeared out the door and back into the meeting room, where he instructed Karl and Betty to leave their luggage. Betty excused herself to refill her ice tea at the snack bar they passed while walking in, feeling her pocket to make sure she still had an adequate supply of Splenda. A man wearing white pants, a button-up bowling shirt, and a straw fedora hat smiled and tilted his hat, saying, "Good morning." She thought he looked just like someone would dress in Miami.

Karl was digging through his bag when the door to the meeting room swung open and two uniquely dressed women entered. "Hello?" Karl said, hesitant to say anything.

"Greetings," June smiled with a strand of braided hair in her eyes. Karl was still staring at her flowered moo-moo and hiking boots.

"Can we help you?" Violet snapped, realizing they were being stared at.

Shaking his head and forcing himself from the trance, Karl forced his eyes back to the bag he was digging into, saying "No, I'm... ok."

"Don't pay attention to her—she's a crappy old thing when it comes to strangers," the other woman said with a laugh. "I'm June; what's your name?" She held out her hand.

"Karl." He shook her hand, thinking she had a man's grip.

"This is Violet, and we are moving here. You?"

"Um, yes. My wife and I are." He let go of her hand. "What brings you to Cedar Branch?" he asked to strike up a conversation.

"We're dying!" Violet blurted out.

"Oh... I'm sorry to hear that," Karl replied, deciding he was in a conversation that he wanted out of.

"We're all dying." June shot daggers at her sister, then looked back at Karl, "Guitar lessons." She smiled in a chipper tone.

Karl cocked his head sideways. "You moved here for guitar lessons?"

"Do you play?" June's voice grew with interest.

"No, no, I don't."

"Oh, OK. Maybe you can join us when we start," June replied.

The door swung back open as Jack walked in removing his fedora hat. "They said this is where the shindig is happening," he blurted out with a grin.

"I haven't heard that, but we can make one," June replied, clueless to what Jack was talking about.

"I'm Jack." He stuck out his hand to Karl.

"Karl."

"I'm June, and this is my crabby sister, Violet," June volunteered.

"Well, hello June and crabby sister, Violet." Jack smiled, keeping the attention of the room.

Turning back to Karl, Jack went on, "So, Karl, you a widower or divorcee like myself? If so, I just passed a babe that would fit you." Karl stuttered for his words as Betty walked back in with her ice tea. "Well, speak of the devil, there she is," Jack replied softly so she couldn't hear.

"Thanks, my wife," Karl snapped in a higher-pitched tone.

Jack pointed at him. "Hey, I'm pretty good at this match making, aren't I?"

Before Karl had a chance to respond, Derrick walked in, announcing himself and welcoming those that were already there. Kat followed, giving the women a softer and more personal welcome with a small gift basket. Jack looked over June's shoulder as she dug into the gift basket, pulling out hand lotion and a small box of locally made chocolate.

"We are still missing someone, but has everyone met everyone?" Derrick asked.

Jack turned to Betty. "Hello, you're the bride of this young gentlemen?" He pointed to Karl.

"I am. Betty Rutherfurd." She shook his hand.

"Jack Goslin," he replied and turned to Violet. "Jack," he introduced himself more formally.

"Jack," Violet replied.

"That is a beautiful blouse," June observed, walking up to Betty.

"Well, thank you, I got it at a small boutique from the town we are from."

"What town is that?" June asked.

"Fairhope, Alabama," Karl interjected.

"Fairhope?" Jack's attention was caught. "Is that diner still there on Church Street?"

"There are two of them. You familiar with Fairhope?" Karl quizzed him.

"Born and raised there. Say, you and I could be kinfolks," Jack answered as Derrick caught his attention to introduce himself.

"Lord, I hope not." Karl replied so only Betty could hear him.

"Behave," she said, smacking him in the arm with the back of her hand.

Everyone was so busy with introductions that they didn't see or hear a mild, meek man enter the room. Gerald set his old hardback suitcase with the others in the corner of the room, then stood silently behind everyone waiting for instructions. Derrick had started to settle down the room and get everyone's attention to explain the week when he saw Gerald standing in the back.

"You must be Mr. Harriman?" Derrick greeted him.

"I am," he softly answered.

"Come meet everyone." Derrick put his arm around Harriman and led him into the group of retirees.

"Jack, this is Gerald," Derrick said, introducing them.

"Hello, Gerald, welcome to the shindig."

"Shindig?" he asked barely loudly enough for Jack to hear.

"Shindig! Party. Gathering... we'll figure it out. Let me introduce you to the Stevens sisters of Camden, Arkansas." He pushed by Derrick.

"OK," Gerald replied.

Chapter 7

After struggling to gain the attention of everyone, Derrick was able to get them settled into their chairs facing each other in a large circle. After quickly introducing himself to Kat, Jack leaned back over to her and made the comment that he felt like he was in an AA meeting. Derrick gave her a funny look at her outburst of laughter and proceeded with the meeting. Walking in and squeezing between two chairs, Simon grabbed his seat and smiled at the group.

"Let's start out by everyone saying their name and where they are from," Derrick said. Instantly four of the six began saying their name, and before they could finish, Derrick broke back in, "Let's start one at a time."

"You got to make that clear," Karl blurted out. Betty tapped his leg, informing him it was OK, Derrick had it. "Well I'm just saying that —" Betty interrupted him again with a glare.

"OK! We are going to start with the leaders, who have prepared a question for everyone to answer so we can get to know you better. Let's start with you." He pointed to Kat.

Her warm smile lit the room. "My name is Katlyn Rose, but everyone calls me Kat."

"Oh, that's a beautiful name," June bellowed out.

"Why can't we call you Rose?" Jack asked. "Like the girl on the *Titanic*."

"She was a fictional character," Karl added.

"You can call me Rose if you like." She grinned at the flirtatious comment. Gerald slowly raised his hand, catching the eye of Kat. "Yes, sir," she pointed.

"Actually, the screenwriter of *Titanic* wrote the character Rose after the artist Beatrice Wood." He settled back in his chair. "And she wasn't on the *Titanic*," he added.

Everyone in the group nodded with the brief history lesson and gave their attention back to Kat. "And I am from New Orleans. I want to add that I am looking forward not only to meeting each one of you, but also spending a wonderful week with you. My question is simple—what is your favorite place to visit?"

"The bathroom!" June blurted out. With everyone looking at her after her weird answer, "Where is the bathroom?" she asked.

"Down the hall," Derrick pointed, and June dismissed herself.

"I'd say the bar," Jack answered.

"No, geographical place," Kat corrected him.

"There are a lot of bars geographically placed," Jack answered.

"Scotland!" Karl interjected, tired of Jack.

"OK. Who else?" Kat asked the rest of the group. Everyone gave their favorite place, with Jack changing his from the bar to Key West. After everyone answered and June made it back to the room, Derrick pointed to Simon.

Simon gave a wave to the group. "I'm Simon, and I'm from Atlanta."

"So if Simon says, we have to do it?" Jack laughed. Karl rolled his eyes.

"No, I'm just the errand boy on this trip," Simon said. "My question is, what are some facts about getting old that I should know?"

Derrick felt his blood pressure rise and quickly butted in. "Let's ask another question that isn't age-related." He gave Simon a strong stare.

"No, I like the question," Violet said. "Hmm, I would have to say everything hurts, and what doesn't hurt, doesn't work." She nodded toward Simon, whose eyes widened at the thought of everything hurting.

"I would say it takes longer to rest than it did to get tired," Betty said before anyone could answer. Derrick tried to regain the attention of the room.

"It takes twice as long to look half as good," June answered. Kat was starting to laugh, not sure if they were being serious. Derrick, still upset with Simon's question, tried to break in, but was cut off by Jack.

"After 81 years I gave up all my bad habits, and I still don't feel well!" Jack answered.

"You don't care where your wife goes, just so you don't have to go along with her," Karl blurted out. Everyone started laughing as Betty slapped his arm again, spilling her ice tea.

"Ok, those are some great answers, but maybe we should ask if—" Derrick started.

"Wait!" Jack interrupted him and looked at Gerald, "What about you?"

Derrick tried to break in again, but was met with Jack's hand signaling him to hush. Gerald swallowed, "Old age? I believe I have more patience," he answered honestly.

Jack lifted one eyebrow. "Do you have more patience, or is it that you just don't care anymore?" He laughed.

Gerald grinned, "Maybe a little of both."

"OK." Derrick started, hoping not to be interrupted again. "My name is Derrick St. Clair. I am from Jacksonville, Florida. My question is, what do you want to see come from this week?" He smiled at his question and faced the quiet group.

"I liked his question," Violet said, pointing at Simon.

Defeated by Simon, Derrick replied, "OK, what are some other facts about becoming a senior?"

"You mean getting old," Karl said. "Another one for me in that my new recliner has more options than my first car." The room livened back up.

"I know that when I got old, I could live without sex, but not without my glasses," June said in a serious tone.

"Do you know I lost my glasses the other day, and it took me a half hour to realize they were on my head?" Betty shook her finger at the group.

As the group started to settle back down, Jack spoke up. "I realized I was old when I would wake up with that morning-after feeling, and I didn't do anything the night before!" Everyone broke back out into laughter, and the answers started flowing again.

As the group blurted out their answers, Derrick leaned over to Simon. "It's not the question I was upset with; we don't want to offend anyone by talking about their age. It might sound like we're calling them old people. Do you understand?" he asked in a milder tone.

"Sure, but I don't think they've forgotten how old they are. Let's give them some fun this week," Simon replied.

"We will," Derrick patted him on the back.

"OK, folks." Derrick stepped out in the middle of the room, "Let's take this conversation and start our tour of the facilities. I know some of you have been here before, but let's take this tour together.

"With this group it will take a week to tour this place," Karl whispered to Betty.

"You're one to talk; it took you two times to get over the speed bump in the parking lot," Betty pointed out.

"I stumbled!" he defended himself.

Chapter 8

Leaving their luggage in the meeting room and gathering their personal belongings, the group headed out the door that Derrick was holding open. Kat and Simon visited with June while Violet scrambled through her purse for her cell phone. Kat, the last one to leave the room, placed her hand on the arm that was holding the door open. "Thank you," she smiled.

The touch of her hand sent chills up Derrick's spine and sparked a debate over asking her to coffee or supper. Cedar Branch had strict rules about co-workers dating and had a history of letting people go who had violated the rule. Derrick wrote off his feelings toward Kat as a crush, not falling for someone, something he had not experienced. He had wondered if she had ever dated because during her few years at Cedar Branch, she had not spoken of anyone.

June caught up with Violet, asking, "Why are you bringing that cell phone? Who are you expecting to call us?"

"I just want it in case Mr. Hettsle calls."

"Why would he call?" June looked at her.

"I don't know." She stepped closer to June. "I'm worried about the booby trap we set in the locked room," she whispered.

Whispering back, June asked, "*Will* you let it go? That military man we talked to about setting booby traps assured us that it would look like an accident if anyone ever entered the room."

Jack stepped in-between the two ladies with his cell phone in hand, commenting "I see you have the same phone. Do you know how to work it?"

"I know how to answer it," Violet replied, hoping he hadn't heard their conversation.

"My assistant gave this one to me before I left and told me it was pretty self-explanatory. I didn't have time to argue with him that self-explanatory and technology didn't exist in my time."

"I bet Kat could show us how to use it," she answered, looking back at her.

With a nod and grin, Jack turned and waited for Kat to catch up with him, then presented her with his dilemma. The first building they came to housed the fitness center and store, and Derrick jogged ahead and opened the door for the group. While a handful of people worked out, the group made their way through the fitness center and into the store.

"Don't you think it's funny that you can work out, then come over here and get your ice-cream?" Gerald said to Derrick, pointing to the coolers.

"I haven't thought of it," he replied, laughing.

With a grin, Gerald answered, "Makes me want to work out."

Violet grabbed two sticks of beef jerky and approached the cashier, eyeing the candy bars that were shelved below the check-out space. The group had made their way out into the covered walkway as Violet finished checking out, giving her time to open one of the beef sticks and catch up.

"That's gonna give you bad breath," her sister replied.

"And?" she questioned June.

"Well, just don't talk too close to someone."

"It'll keep people from invading my bubble." Violet chewed off a piece, showing her teeth. June shook her head and walked on with the group that was heading to the Tower apartments. A light breeze passed through them, blowing a piece of paper from Kat's clipboard onto the grass.

Stepping off the walkway to retrieve the paper, Betty stopped to wait on her. "Tell me about you," Betty said as Kat stepped back on the walkway.

"My life is simple, I enjoy work and outdoor things," Kat answered.

"Are you single?" Betty went straight to the point.

"Yes, ma'am, I am."

Betty pointed at Derrick that was leading the pack. "Is he single?"

Kat smiled, replying that "Cedar Branch has a strong policy about employees dating."

"But is he single?"

"I believe so." The thought entered Kat's mind for the first time.

Karl butted in their conversation. "Why are we going to the apartments? He's not going to show where everyone is going to live, is he?"

"We'll just pass through the lobby; he might tell what floor you live on," Kat answered.

"I don't want all these people to know where I am going to live!" Karl barked.

Kat didn't know how to reply to the comment; at Cedar Branch, most people knew where everyone lived. They followed the group into the formal lobby with commercial-grade carpet and concrete statues of Greek gods welcoming residents. Derrick stopped in the center and began explaining how the Tower was not on the initial plans, but with the popularity of Cedar Branch, the architects drew it in, causing it to be the most-wanted place to live.

Pulling out his clip board, "Most of you have reserved apartments here. The Stevens sisters will be living on the third floor. And The Rutherfurd's and Mr. Goslin are on the fifth." Derrick recited.

Karl's face turned red. "I told you I don't want everyone to know where we are going to live!" he whispered to Betty.

"Karl, within a week everyone is going to know where we live."

"And now, to make things worse, I have to live next to that jackass!" He nonchalantly pointed at Jack, who was making his way to them.

"Well, neighbor," Jack smiled, "looks like we will be seeing a lot of each other."

"Looks that way." Karl was without any other words.

Jack turned to Gerald. "Gerald, my man, where are you living?"

Gerald pointed through the wall and in the direction of the adjacent building, "I have a place at the Loft apartments. I didn't need anything too big."

"You're just a hop, skip, and a jump over." Jack made his way back to Karl. "Gerald is sure a surreptitious man. I wonder what he's hiding," he said under his breath for only Karl to hear.

"Surreptitious?" Karl turned to Betty for the definition. She smiled and walked on with the group, leaving Karl to guess what the word meant. He grinned at Jack, trying to give the impression that he understood what he was talking about.

The tour continued through the Loft apartments, the Charleston apartments, indoor pool, chapel, and outdoor facilities before ending where they started. Jack gave his cell phone back to Kat, showing her that something had appeared on the screen. "You have a text message from your son," she said.

"What's it say?"

"He is checking in and making sure you're staying out of trouble." She looked at him. "Sounds like your son knows you well," she smiled.

"You'd be surprised," he answered, taking the phone and leaving her questioning the comment.

Chapter 9

Once back in the meeting room, everyone found their luggage had already been loaded in the van and a cooler of bottled water and snacks were set out. Violet and Karl walked out to the van looking for their bags as the group grabbed water and snacks for the drive. Derrick walked out to make sure Karl was finding his bag and found that Violet had already unloaded the van and was analyzing the bags for weight and size.

"Ms. Stevens, do you need help?" he asked.

Lifting a heavy brown leather suitcase, Violet responded, "I'm making sure it's loaded properly. If the back is not balanced, the van could get squirrely."

Confused, Derrick looked at Karl, and on eye contact Karl circled his ear with his index figure, insinuating she was crazy. Karl finished digging out his fanny pack and walked back in the meeting room.

Not interested in confronting Violet with the question of balancing the van, Derrick started loading the bags. "Point to bags you think should go where and I'll load them."

Violet smiled at his willingness and pointed to a bag. "Put that one on the left side and we'll stack another on top."

Simon walked out. "You're repacking the van?" he asked.

"Yep, give me a hand," Derrick said from inside.

"Hand him that one next," Violet ordered, pointing at another bag, and before long the balancing team had successfully packed the van.

After loading the last bag, Simon headed back inside, holding the door open for Violet to follow and Kat to come out with a bottle of water for Derrick. "That was sweet," she said, handing him a bottle of water.

"Thanks." He took the water, adding, "I learned early not to argue, plus it's their trip, not ours."

They joined everyone inside, who were curiously watching the young couple talk. Betty gave Kat a big smile as they entered. "You guys ready for a great week? Last chance for a bathroom for a short time." Derrick barely got the words out before losing everyone to the bathroom but Gerald.

"Mr. Harriman, are you excited?" Kat asked, breaking the silence, but receiving only a simple "yes." She smiled back at Derrick, then gathered her things. Soon the group was back in the room, with Jack being the last one.

"Ok! Let's go!" Derrick opened the door.

Karl and Betty climbed in first and made their way to the back seat, followed by Gerald. "Hang on!" Violet yelled. The group froze and turned to her. "There is no way this van is going to make it if we don't balance it out the right way."

"What?" Karl looked at Betty.

"I think she wants everyone to sit in certain places."

"What the hell does it matter?" Karl yelled from the back of the van.

Violet looked at Derrick. "Who's driving?" Confused, he pointed at himself. "Ok, then Jack and Gerald sit in the back, June and I will take the middle, and Karl, Betty, and Simon take the front. That leaves Derrick driving and Kat in the passenger side."

"What the hell does it matter?" Karl yelled again, this time receiving an elbow from Betty.

Kat stepped in, saying "After you, gentlemen." She held her hand toward the van, looking at Jack and Gerald, who gladly stepped in, followed by the sisters, leaving Karl, Betty, Simon, and Kat on the driveway. "Simon? You and I weigh about the same," Kat said loud enough for Violet to hear. "I'll sit with the Rutherfurd's."

"But we left the front for you to sit next to Derrick," June blurted out.

Catching the sister's idea about trying to match-make her and Derrick, Kat said, "I'll sit up there some during the week."

"So if someone eats more than they should, is that going to screw-up the seating assignments?" Karl snarled.

"You'll be the first to know," Betty retorted.

Finally on the road, Derrick plugged in his smart phone to the radio and tuned into the Frank Sinatra station. Kat grinned at the thoughtful jester and simple things he had thought of to make everyone's trip comfortable and fun. Little did she know that he was a Frank Sinatra fan. Kat dug in her brief case and brought out a laminated agenda for their week, and Karl looked on, not wanting to pull his agenda out of his back pocket.

"First stop is the art museum," she announced to the group.

Jack turned to Gerald. "Tell me about yourself," he said, getting the attention of the sisters.

"Not a whole lot to tell," Gerald softly replied.

"Single? Widower? Retired from?" Jack gave him examples. June turned to better hear his answers.

"Doris passed away eight months ago. I was in the hotel business most of my life. What else?" He looked up in thought, "I'm a Kenny Rogers fan." He shrugged his shoulders, not knowing what else to say.

"You got a picture of Doris?" June asked.

"I do." He gladly opened his bag and pulled out the framed 8X10 picture.

"That's a big picture to carry around all the time," Karl said, looking on.

"My son tried showing me how to put pictures on my cell phone, but it's just not the same," Gerald replied.

"You keep carrying that 8X10 and don't let anyone tell you different. I think that's romantic." Jack rested his arm on the seat behind Gerald and patted him on the back.

"Romantic? What the hell does he know about romance?" Karl said for only Betty to hear.

"Not everyone is as romantic as you are, sweetie." She rolled her eyes.

"Damn right," he answered.

Only a few miles down the interstate, a loud explosion came from under the van, and with a jerk of the steering wheel, Derrick veered into the right lane and onto the shoulder of the interstate. "What was that?" Karl yelled.

"Flat tire," Derrick calmly replied [...] shoulder.

"Do you want me to call someone?" Kat [...]

"Nah, it's just a flat tire. It won't take long t[...] He set the parking brake, adding, "Simon, will y[...] a hand with the luggage? The tire is under all of it[...]

"How many times are we going to pack this van?" [...] asked, sliding out of his seat.

"Everyone stay inside. This will only take a minute," Derrick responded, smiling at the retirees, and before he could close his door, Karl, Jack, Gerald, and Violet climbed out.

Setting the first bag down, Derrick noticed he and Simon weren't the only ones outside of the van. Since the interstate wasn't busy, he figured it wouldn't hurt to have everyone out of the van. The four of them stood in the grass just far enough out of the way and watched the two men unload the van to get to the spare tire and tools to change it. As Simon knelt down and placed the jack under the frame in the slot that was meant for it, Karl was the first to say something.

"You need to put that under the axle," he insisted, "or you'll bend the body and possibly the frame." Taking a step back and examining the van on the road, he added, "It looks level enough, though."

"Actually the new vans have a slot for the jack on the side. The manufacturer made it so that it would be safer," Derrick educated Karl.

Simon began turning the handle, making the screw jack rise up. Jack was next on advice. "You need a wooden block to go between the jack and frame."

"Then the jack won't fit in the slot," Simon replied.

"Put it under the jack," Karl insisted, with Jack agreeing.

"I don't have a block of wood," Simon answered.

"Fan out! I bet there's one somewhere here on the side of the road," Violet said, waving her arms.

Simon started laughing and looked at Derrick. "Maybe we'll have it changed before they find a piece of wood."

Gerald stayed with Derrick and Simon while the others kicked the tall grass searching for a mythical piece of wood. Simon felt someone standing over him while he worked the jack, "Yes sir?" He turned to find Gerald looking down with his hands on his knees.

"Are you going to chock the front tires?" he asked.

"I believe Derrick set the parking brake."

"I'll find something just in case," Gerald replied, and he too began searching in the grass.

As quickly as any race car pit crew, Derrick and Simon had the tire changed and half the bags reloaded before the others realized they didn't wait on them. Violet raised one of her eyebrows. "Are you putting them in the way we had them?" She nodded to the luggage.

"Yes, ma'am," Simon answered, looking at Derrick and hoping they were; he knew they'd be unloading them if not.

"What in the world were y'all doing kicking the grass around?" Betty asked them.

"Looking for a block," Karl answered, squeezing by her.

"It looked like you were hunting Easter eggs," she replied.

Karl just grunted at her comment. "Simon!" June yelled over everyone.

Simon turned as he buckled his seat belt, "Yes ma'am?"

"That's another one for your question about getting old."

"What's that?"

"We old folks can hide our own Easter eggs!"

Kat laughed, "Simon, you need to be taking notes on this."

"I need to write a book about this week," Simon laughed.

"Now that's a good idea. Are you a writer?" June asked him.

"I write for fun, nothing serious." He dropped the conversation.

Betty pulled out her notepad, saying "I always carry mine." She proudly showed the van.

"For not forgetting things," Karl blurted out.

The van raced down the interstate toward the museum, losing hardly any time with the flat tire. As Gerald sat in the back watching the cars heading in the opposite direction and looking into the sky, he began to drift to a place nine months earlier. He found himself sitting in a hospital room next to the woman he loved. She barely had enough strength to hold his hand. Asking for ice, Gerald received a cup of crushed ice and fed it gently to her with a spoon.

The doctors had given her only a month to live 12 weeks earlier, leaving Gerald only to wait for his love to move on without him. He had watched her body become more and more fragile, with her heart slowly dying. It was on a warm winter day when the grip of Doris's hand slipped out of Gerald's, starting a new chapter in his life, one that he was beginning at Cedar Branch.

The van came to a gentle stop in front of the museum just as Gerald was wakening from his daydream. "Well,

Gerald, let's go see what some paintings have to say," Jack said, pulling himself up from their seat. Stepping out of the van, he noticed a hotdog cart on the corner that lured him in without saying anything to anyone.

The group congregated at the door as Derrick parked the van, making his way back to the group. "Where's Jack?"

Three of the five pointed to the hotdog cart with Jack leaning on the cart talking with the vendor. "Jack! You ready?" Derrick yelled to hurry him up. Jack held up an index finger while eating his dog with the other. "You guys go ahead; I'll get him," Derrick said.

"Jack-ass wants us to wait on him," Karl whispered to Betty as the group walked in the modern white concrete building.

"You want one?" Jack asked Derrick.

"No, thank you. We better catch up with the rest of the group."

Wiping his mouth with a napkin, Jack replied, "Yea, you're probably right. Tony! Great dog, I'll be back." Then Jack said, "Derrick! What's it going to take to get you and Kat together?"

"What? Kat? Why would you... ."

"Oh relax, your secret is safe with me."

"I don't have a secret," Derrick defended himself.

Jack stopped and looked at him, "Son, I've been married five times and dated a lot of women. I see how you look at her and treat her. If you're interested, ask her out."

"I'm not interested," Derrick said, "Plus Cedar Branch has a strict policy about dating co-workers."

"You know what policies are for? Breaking!" Jack started walking again, "You can't policy love!"

Derrick smiled at his words and held the door open for him. "I'll tell you what—if I get interested in her, I'll talk to you."

"Then I'll meet you at the hot dog stand after this." Jack replied, walking up to the group.

Kat gathered everyone in a group, saying "I would like to introduce you to your tour guide." She spun around, held her arms out, and continued. "Me! I have always appreciated the fine arts and have visited this gallery many times. I hope I don't bore you, so follow me." She smiled and turned, flipping her light brown hair to the side. Jack looked back to Derrick, who seemed to be paralyzed by his glance at Kat.

"We might be getting two dogs with that stare," Jack responded, pulling Derrick out of his trance.

Chapter 11

Sitting at the table, Betty searched her purse for the spare Splendas she kept in the side pocket while everyone gabbed about the museum and made the daunting decision of ordering lunch. Violet, who had tuned out the group's conversation, stared at her cell phone impatiently, waiting on their attorney to return her call. He had never been hard to get a hold of on the phone, and this was the third message she had left him.

Jack had chosen the seat at the head of the table and had rested his fedora hat on the end. He and June were deep into a conversation about a piece at art they both liked. Karl piped up about a copy of Van Gogh's *Starry Night* and made a statement that the original was painted while he studied the stars.

"Actually, Van Gogh painted it from his second story room in an asylum he was staying in—it's a painting of the village that was just out his window," Gerald replied, leaning over to see Karl.

With a smirk, Karl argued, "I'm pretty sure it was done outside."

Looking at the rest of the table, Gerald added to his history lesson. "He painted it 21 times before coming up with the masterpiece." Everyone acknowledged Gerald's information, leaving Karl mumbling something under his breath.

"Tell you what, Gerald, after we get settled in at Cedar Branch, you and I need to head to the Big Apple and visit the original." Jack held his glass of water up.

"That would be nice," Gerald replied, intrigued with the invitation.

A young waitress returned to the table to take their order. "Sweetheart, what would you recommend?" Jack asked, studying his menu.

"I thought you weren't hungry," Karl snapped.

"I wasn't, but the charm from this young lady changed my mind." He winked at her.

Karl rolled his eyes and pulled his menu close enough to read without his glasses. After the group had taken more time ordering their lunch than it did to tour the museum, they handed their menus to the waitress and continued their conversations.

June's phone began ringing in her hand, "Are you going to get that?" Violet looked at her sister.

June looked at her phone surprised, that she didn't hear it. "Hello?" she answered the number she didn't recognize.

"Ms. Stevens?" the voice asked.

"Yes."

"This is Chief Baker with the Camden Police Department."

June left her seat, walking to the door so she could hear better. "How can I help you?" she was puzzled at the call.

"I'm not sure how to tell you this over the phone, but there has been an accident at your house," the chief replied.

"Accident? We are not at home."

"Yes, ma'am, I understand. You and your sister are friends with Jimmy Hettsle?"

"We are. He is our attorney."

"Did he have permission to enter your house?" the chief asked.

"Yes. We asked him to watch the house while we are making a move to a retirement community. Is he OK?"

"No, ma'am, I'm sorry to say he passed away this morning in your house. One of your neighbors saw him enter the house and walked to the yard, where they heard a loud noise coming from the inside and called authorities. It turns out that part of the flooring in the house collapsed, and Mr. Hettsle fell to his death."

June's body went numb, as she knew the only weak place in the floor of their house was in the locked room, the room with the very booby trap she and her sister had made.

"Ms. Stevens, he was in a locked room where my officers found quite a bit of cash. I assume he was checking on your savings?" The chief's voice had a hint of interrogation.

Not knowing what to say, June replied, "Yes, he often checked on our savings."

"Can I send an officer to pick you and your sister up to come collect your money and ask a few more—"

June hung up the phone, blurting out, "Oh, dear God! We've killed our attorney!" She rushed back to the table and pulled on Violet. "We need to talk." The sisters disappeared outside.

"I hope everything is OK," Gerald commented, watching them quickly vanish out the door.

Betty turned the attention on Kat with her question, "Kat, tell us more about you."

Kat smiled, not interested in talking about herself. "Like I mentioned earlier, I live a simple life," she responded, hoping that was sufficient.

"What outside things do you like to do?" Betty asked, remembering their conversation.

"I don't know where to start. I love everything about the outdoors. I enjoy hiking and backpacking, and I own a kayak, so I love the water too."

Derrick looked up at the sound of kayak, since he owned one too. Jack took notice of his sudden acknowledgment and sparked a question, putting Derrick on the spot. "Do you own a kayak too?"

"I do," Derrick answered, wondering how he knew that.

Looking at him, Kat replied, "I didn't know that."

"Where's your family?" Betty continued questioning her.

"Born in New Orleans, but we moved to a small town in north Georgia while I was still young, and they are still there. I moved after college to Perdido Bay to start my career." Her memory drifted back to the day she moved. Kat had dated one guy during her college years, Monty. They had a great relationship, and several times Kat had thought about marriage and wondered if Monty was the right guy. In their senior year, though, Monty began changing and becoming more controlling and over protective of her, her time, and her friends.

During a spring night, Kat told Monty she was going out with a few of her girlfriends. It was then she realized his obsession with her was getting out of hand. He demanded that she stay home in a rage, a rage she had never seen before, and when she disagreed with him, a fight broke out that ended their relationship—but not ending the countless times Monty called, showed up at her apartment, and followed her wherever she went. Her mother begged her to call the police and file a report, but Kat believed that he would eventually stop. With the stalking getting worse, she made a move without leaving a trace of where she moved, Perdido Bay.

"Don't you think?" Betty asked Kat, drawing her out of her trance.

"What?" She had missed the question.

"You two should go kayaking." Betty pointed at Derrick, who was a light shade of red.

"We should." She smiled at Derrick, leaving him blushing.

Chapter 12

Sitting on the table in front of Derrick was a basket of beignets with Simon just beyond the warm bread. June walked back in the restaurant without Violet and sat at her seat while everyone stared in curiosity. Karl looked throughout the table to see who would generate the question. Without waiting, he asked "Where's Violet?"

"She is getting some fresh air," June replied, dropping her napkin in her lap.

"Fresh air?"

"A friend of ours passed away today," she replied without looking up.

"Oh, sorry," Karl answered, guilty of being nosey.

Before anyone could ask any other questions, their waitress returned with a serving tray balanced on her shoulder. She presented everyone with their plates and set down a soup and sandwich in Violet's empty place.

"Maybe we should let Violet know her food is here," Betty commented, but June didn't make any movement to respond to the remark. "Karl, go see if she'll come eat," Betty suggested.

"I'm sure she'll come in when she's ready," he replied with a mouth full.

Betty set her napkin on her plate and slid back from the table, but Karl stopped her chair and wiped his mouth. "I'll go," he huffed.

"Do you mind going with Karl?" Derrick asked Simon, who replied with a simple "OK."

Walking out, they were met with a busy sidewalk with people waiting their turn to be seated. Karl walked out and looked both ways. "I don't see her," he said, and started back in the restaurant.

"I bet she went this way," Simon walked in front of the restaurant.

"How do you know she went this way?"

"I don't know, just figured."

"My lunch is getting cold," Karl started to argue.

"Go eat. I'll find her."

"Wait up." Karl knew if he went back alone he would get the third degree from his wife. They walked looking in the small shops that lined the street and across the busy two-lane street. After making it several blocks, Karl spotted an empty bench resting against a store front and sat down mumbling something about missing his lunch. Simon noticed he was alone and walked back to the bench to sit down.

"How long have you worked for the retirement community?" Karl asked.

"Three months."

"Are you finished with college?"

"No, I made it a year and decided it wasn't for me."

"What made you want to work for Cedar Branch?"

"They had an opening," Simon answered, scanning the street.

"Well, what do you want to do for a career?" Karl pressed.

"I don't know. I figure something will pop up."

Pop up! Great, Karl thought to himself, *our trip is being co-led by a member of the Scooby Doo gang.* "You got to have a plan! Is there anything you want to do?" Karl continued.

"I like writing and would like to be a journalist. But most places want a degree in something, and I don't want to spend four years in school learning nothing that would prepare me for that."

"Nothing? I wouldn't say school was a waste. Places want to hire someone that has put forth an effort to learn the essentials."

"Maybe we should head back," Simon suggested, not wanting to be preached to about school.

"Give me a minute to rest," Karl asked.

"Let's get a cab to take us back." Simon waved down a cab before Karl could say anything. Pulling himself up, Karl squeezed between two parked cars and into the back seat of the taxi, followed by Simon. The driver motioned for destination without speaking.

"Fresh Baked Café," Simon answered.

The driver accelerated, jumping back in line with the traffic and causing Simon's phone to fall on the floorboard under Karl's feet. Karl reached down, but before he reached the phone, the driver took a hard right off the street that led back to their restaurant. Simon slid in his seat, pinning Karl between the door and Simon.

"Where in the hell is this driver going?" Karl said, pushing Simon back to his side of the cab.

"Short cut," Simon shrugged his shoulders.

"Where are you going?" Karl asked the driver.

"Bakery!" The driver replied in a thick Middle Eastern accent.

"Bakery? We need to go to a restaurant called Fresh Baked!" Karl snapped.

"Sorry. No English." The driver handed them a map to point to their destination.

"No English!" Karl shouted. "We're in America!" His voice trembled as Simon started laughing. "What's so funny? I'm missing my lunch!"

"We've been cab jacked by a driver that can't speak English."

"And that's funny?"

"Don't worry." Simon leaned over the seat, "Do you speak Spanish?"

"Ce." The driver's expression lit up.

"*Restaurante hornear fresca?*" Simon said the restaurant's name in Spanish.

"Ce!" The cab took another hard left, causing Karl to slide into Simon.

"That figures! A foreigner taxi driver that can't speak English, but knows a language that isn't his own," Karl grumbled.

"There she is." Simon pointed through the window at Violet appearing from a store across the street with a small bag.

"You can stop!" Karl barked at the driver, who just stared at him through the rear-view mirror. "Alto!" Simon yelled.

The tires squealed with the driver stepping hard on the brakes and slamming Karl and Simon into the seat back. Opening the door into traffic, Karl shouted, "Let me out of this God-forsaken death trap!"

The driver yelled at Karl to watch for cars and to get back in the cab. But even if Karl knew the language he was speaking, there was no way he was climbing back in the cab. Simon quickly paid the driver and hopped out.

Violet stopped at the commotion coming from the street with horns being blown and people shouting for the cab to move. Karl walked up to her and said the only thing that came to his mind: "Our lunch is getting cold!"

"Well, that is a different approach to come tell me." She looked over at her shoulder at the driver waving his arm at the two passengers.

"It's a difficult story," Karl snapped and walked back to the restaurant with Simon and Violet in tow.

Entering the restaurant, they found everyone had finished eating with their plates still sitting in place. "We didn't want you to miss lunch," Kat greeted Violet.

"Oh, it's OK. I'm not hungry," she politely answered with the thought of policemen storming the restaurant for the two hardened criminals that had killed their lawyer. She looked at June, who was sitting behind an empty plate as if she had no worries in the world.

Karl stood in place with his jaw on the ground. "Not hungry?" Betty pulled him down to his seat before he could say anything else.

Changing the conversation, Jack asked Kat about the play while leaning back in his seat. "What are we going to see?"

"It is called 'Elvis Again.' It has received great reviews."

Patting Karl on his shoulder, Betty asked, "Did you and Simon get to talk?"

"We've put the life of our trip in the hands of someone who falls between Shaggy Rogers from Scooby Doo and Frankie Avalon," he grumbled, taking a bite of his lunch.

Ignoring the comment, she turned her attention to Jack. "How did you like living in New York?"

"The Big Apple?" He sat up, engaged in the question. "I liked it—it's not the South with the hospitality and pride in frying everything we eat, but it had a good side."

"What did you do there?" Betty asked about his career.

"Real estate."

"Residential?" she asked.

"No, mostly commercial."

"I bet that's a hard area to make a living." Karl piped up with a mouth full, "Is that why you moved back to the South?" He tried cornering Jack about not being the guy that was the center of attention.

"No, I retired. Gave the firm to my son."

"Firm?" Betty asked.

"I had the second largest firm in the city," Jack replied.

Karl made a grunting noise and went back to eating.

Chapter 13

"I'm not sure who is harder to corral—the group or Simon," Kat observed, looking at Simon, who was wandering clueless in the street texting on his phone. Derrick smiled at her comment.

The group had gathered behind Kat while she retrieved the tickets to the play from the box office. June and Violet stood beside each other whispering about their predicament and planning their story to match about the weakness in their floor. Back in Camden, Arkansas, the chief of police never gave the hang up a second thought, given the quirky behavior the sisters demonstrated from time to time.

"Where were you when Elvis made it big?" Jack patted Gerald on the back.

With a soft smile, Gerald answered, "I think I was working for my family, wishing I could catch the girls like Elvis."

"I bet you had to beat the ladies off of you in your younger days," Jack grinned.

"Still do," Gerald grinned back.

Laughing, Jack replied, "Gerald, you and I are going to be good buds!"

Kat handed everyone a single ticket while instructing them of their seats down front and center. With Jack and Gerald in their conversation, she handed her ticket that was beside Jack to Gerald and kept the one that was beside Derrick.

Scuffing his feet against the tile floor, Simon walked up. "King of Rock!" he exclaimed, catching the attention of Betty.

"Oh yes, I can still remember sitting in front of the TV and watching him sing "Jailhouse Rock," she replied with a twinkle in her eye.

"He put his pants on no different than I do," Karl answered with a hint of jealousy.

She grabbed his arm, replying, "Yes, honey, he did," then shot a smile at Kat.

Giggling, Kat turned to the group, "You guys ready?" She started leading them inside.

They walked into a cold and dimly lit auditorium that was already half full of people with the music of Elvis quietly playing to fill the background noise. Betty slipped into her sweater before squeezing in the aisle of chairs and finding her seat. All nine of them filed into the row out of order of their seats and spent the next few minutes climbing over each other to get to their chairs. Karl rolled his eyes at Betty and started to say something, but was cut off with her patting his hand and replying that everything was going to be OK.

Derrick stayed standing until the last one sat and then sank into his red velvet chair beside Kat. After a few minutes, he looked down the row at everyone looking at their phones. "Looks like a bunch of teenagers," he whispered to Kat.

"And half of them don't know how to use them," she said with a smile, looking at Jack, who was still trying to figure out how to text.

"I am sorry to hear about your friend passing," Betty consoled Violet.

"Passing?" she answered, confused.

"June said you had a friend that died."

Startled with the question, she turned to June, who was listening, "Our attorney had an accident," June answered for her.

"That is sad. Did he have family?" Betty asked.

The sisters looked at each other, not knowing the answer—they had never visited with him about his personal life. "Camden is a small town, so everyone has family of some sort," June answered.

"Well, I hope everyone is doing OK." Betty dropped the conversation.

Violet leaned into June, whispering, "What if we killed a family man?"

"He wasn't a family man," June guessed. Her phone rang with a call, and looking down, she said, "Speaking about home." June showed the screen to Violet with the Chief's number displayed.

"Hello?" June answered, squeezing back out of the aisle and walking toward the doors. Violet sat in her seat, trembling of the thought of her sister talking to the police.

"Ms. Stevens? We were cut off while talking about the tragedy that happened here. Can you talk?" the Chief asked.

"I can."

"It might be best if you and your sister come in to answer a few questions and handle the repairs of your home."

"OK? We are actually on a trip for the next week." Her expression squinted as she puzzled over giving the chief their whereabouts.

"I understand. I can have my officers lock up the house and keep a close eye on it until you can get here. As I explained earlier there was a lot of cash in the room, and I would feel safer if we kept it here at the station locked up."

Relieved, June answered, "That would be extremely helpful."

"Ms. Stevens, you should think about putting all that money in the bank."

"Banks get robbed all the time."

"Well, they have insurance on cases like that. But there hasn't been a bank robbery here in 60 years."

"Sounds like you're due for one. Tell me, Chief, did Mr. Hettsle have family?"

The Chief frowned. "No, he didn't. Just call when you and your sister can come in." He turned to an officer that was leaning over his desk. "Those are two crazy women," he said, hanging up the phone.

"You're not going to have them come in?" the officer asked.

"Nah, Hettsle was about as crooked as they come. He probably would have been knocked off if he hadn't had this accident," the chief replied, walking out of his office.

June took a deep breath and walked back into the auditorium as the light dimmed to darkness. With the stage lights slowly illuminating, she found their aisle and squeezed back into her seat. "What did he say?" Violet asked, chomping at the bit.

"They're on the way with SWAT. We better head to the border," she whispered back to Violet. Violet sprang to her feet, catching the attention of everyone. June pulled her back into her seat. "I'm just kidding. They want us to come in when we have a chance. They expect nothing."

Violet took a deep breath with her hand over her heart. "And he wasn't a family man," June added.

Derrick and Kat simultaneously leaned over to watch Violet sit back in her seat and then smiled at each other before focusing back on the stage. Derrick secretly glanced back at Kat, the stage lights reflecting off her facial features and illuminating her eyes. Falling into a semi-trance, he stared out of the corner of his eye. *She is so attractive! Maybe I should ignore this policy and ask her out.*

She sensed the stare and met his eyes with a warm, inviting smile. *I wonder what he's thinking.* Looking back at the stage, she thought *stupid policy*!

Chapter 14

After the first act, Gerald stood up and scooted through the isle. "Where are you heading?" Jack asked.

"Men's room," Gerald whispered.

Jack put on the hat that was resting in his lap and pulled himself up to follow Gerald. Walking up the aisle, he tipped his hat to a couple of young ladies who smiled back. Entering the lobby, Gerald aimed to the left without stopping. "Have you been here before?" Jack asked.

"No, first time."

"You seem to know your way around," Jack said. Gerald looked at him, confused. "You know where the bathrooms are," Jack pointed to the men's door.

"No. Just makes sense they would put them near the snack bar."

"You have a gift of knowing where you are. You would make a good navigator," Jack responded.

Entering the bathroom, Gerald began explaining how navigators used the stars and the instruments they used. Jack counted the tiles on the wall in front of the urinal to block out Gerald's lesson on the stars while he peed. Washing his hands, Jack interrupted the lesson. "Are you a big Elvis fan?" he asked.

Shaking his head, "Not really," Gerald replied.

"Me either, I need to get a few things. Do you want to head down the street to a shop?" Jack said.

Without answering or giving any input, Gerald followed him out onto the sidewalk and toward a small, locally owned men's clothing store. Jack led, tipping his hat at every lady that he passed, with Gerald struggling to keep up. He held the door open to a store for Gerald and stepped in behind him.

A young man approached them, asking "May I help you gentlemen?"

"Socks," Jack replied.

The man smiled and turned, saying "This way."

"I'm not looking for just any socks—I prefer Italian."

The man turned with a bigger smile. "Cotton, wool, or cashmere?"

"Cotton, but I could pick up a couple of cashmere pairs too."

The store was small, but intimate, with dark wooden floors and copper tile ceiling. The two older men were led to a back corner that displayed a variety of high-end socks. Gerald gasped at one of the price tags. Not waiting on the man to describe the brands or explain the materials, Jack grabbed four pair of cotton and two pair of cashmere socks.

"Did you not pack any socks?" Gerald asked, holding two pair for him.

"I never wear a pair twice." Jack replied. The young salesman smiled bigger at him. "Sorry, just passing through," Jack said and walked toward the checkout counter.

"That will be $154.36." The salesman announced after ringing up the sale.

"For socks? That you're going to wear once?" Gerald spoke louder than he had all trip.

"You only live once," Jack answered, pulling out cash.

"What do you do with them once you wear them?"

"Give 'em away."

"I'll be glad to be your charitable recipient," Gerald offered with a grin.

Jack took the sack from the salesman and laughed at Gerald's offer. "Let's find a book store," he said, walking toward the door.

Back at the play, Kat looked at her watch then at Derrick. "Should we go see if they are all right?"

"Maybe so," Derrick replied, looking toward the door to see if Jack and Gerald had come back in. Violet and June took the opportunity of Derrick's leaving and headed out with him, aiming towards the ladies room.

Betty sat up and watched the women leaving and then turned back to Karl, saying, "I need some air."

"OK," Karl whispered back, not taking his eyes off the performer.

Once Betty made it out, Kat leaned over to Karl. "Is everyone all right?"

"Betty went for fresh air."

Kat waited a couple of minutes for the song to end and the lights to go down before she headed out of the theater, leaving Karl and Simon in the aisle of seats. The sunlight blasting through the windows in the lobby blinded her momentarily until she gained her bearings of where Betty had gone. A small court yard with the shade from an old oak tree was tucked in the back corner of the theater. Betty was sitting on one of the benches. "Do you mind if I join you?" Kat said in a soft voice.

Betty's face warmed with a smile. "Not at all. But you're missing the show."

"It's OK," she said, sitting down beside her.

A welcoming light breeze made its way through the court yard, cooling off the area. The ladies watched as a large group of people used the court yard as a shortcut. "Tell me about you," Kat invited.

Before Betty could say anything, the Stevens sisters appeared from the small door that led to the lobby. "Are we interrupting?" June asked.

"Absolutely not," Betty answered. June and Violet sat at a small white iron table with two chairs, and Kat noticed that Violet was not as talkative as she had been.

"Are you doing OK?" Kat asked Violet.

"I'm fine." Violet tried to hide that her thoughts were focused on home. "Y'all didn't like the show?"

"Yes, I just needed a bit of fresh air."

"Us too. Plus after seeing the real Elvis, it's hard to watch an impersonator," June replied.

"Where did you see him?" Kat asked, interested.

"The Hayride Kitchen in Shreveport. It's where he got his start. He was a heart throb back then." June waved her shirt back and forth.

Laughing, Betty asked, being nosey, "I know you were not married, but was there ever a man in your life?"

"Not that lived up to par," Violet answered.

"Maybe one will come along," Kat replied.

Violet paused with a smirk, saying, "Sweetheart, I'm 83—he'd better hurry!"

Just then Jack and Gerald walked in the court yard. "Ladies!" Jack tipped his hat. The four of them burst into laughter, and Jack and Gerald looked at each other puzzled about the unusual welcome. Jack looked at his zipper. "Are my pants unzipped?" The laughter got louder, and the two men had no choice but to join in.

"Looks like I'm missing the party," Derrick commented, walking in behind the men. Betty cut her eyes at Kat and elbowed her, but Kat pushed her arm down while turning a light shade of red.

Chapter 15

Once everyone loaded into the van under the guidance of Violet and the complaints from Karl, the group headed to their hotel. The streets were busy with shoppers and those who had attended the show, causing traffic to crawl. Everyone sat quietly in their places with Gerald nodding off to sleep beside Jack. "I need to stop for fuel before we get to the hotel," Derrick commented, looking at Kat in the rear-view mirror.

A cell phone buzzed from the back of the van, growing louder and louder. Kat turned to see Jack staring out the window. "Jack, is that your phone?" she asked.

Jack felt his pockets, pulling out his phone. "Sorry." He studied the screen, "This text crap is crazy. Just call if you want to tell me something," he added, talking to his phone.

"Do you need help?" Kat grinned.

Still looking at his phone, Jack replied, "Yea, I believe so."

Kat climbed out of her seat and slipped to the back of the van. Jack scooted closer to Gerald to give Kat room to sit. A sudden gasp of air came from the middle seat, and Kat looked up to see Violet speechless at the audacity of her un-balancing the van. "I'll only be a minute, plus we're not going very fast," she said to try to ease the nerves of Violet.

"It's not that we're going fast. It's the fact that we are now putting extra weight on the back left tire, causing it to wear quicker," Violet blurted out.

Karl turned in his seat before Betty could corral him, "That's the dumbest thing I've ever heard!"

"Are you a tire engineer?" Violet shot back at him.

"A what?" Karl's voice skipped during the question. Betty now had a firm grip on his left arm, doing her best to pull him around.

"I'm not an expert, but I know that they build tires to hold all kinds of weight," Jack chimed in.

"It's about balance, not weight," Violet defended herself.

Jack looked at Gerald, who was awake with all the fuss. "Can you give us some expertise on the friction of tires?" Jack asked.

Violet glared in Gerald's direction. "Nope," he shook his head, looking at the harsh stare from Violet.

"Actually that is the spare tire, so it didn't have as much wear on it as the right side, so we should be OK," Derrick diplomatically replied.

Before anyone could respond to the statement, Betty piped up. "Oh dear! I think I left my glasses in the courtyard."

Derrick looked at Karl and Betty in the rear-view mirror. "We can turn around and go get them."

Karl lowered his eyebrows with a smirk, pulled her glasses off her head, and handed them to her. She innocently smiled, saying "Never mind."

After Kat gave Jack another quick lesson on texting, she made her way back to her seat as the van gained speed merging into traffic on the interstate. Simon turned the radio up to hear a symphony playing in the speakers. "Are you a classics guy?" Derrick questioned him on his music.

"Nah, I just like movie scores."

With everyone settled, Kat leaned in between Derrick and Simon. "I'm a Celtic symphony fan myself," she butted into their conversation.

"I can do some Celtic," Simon replied. The three of them continued the conversation of music, books, and movies as their destination grew closer. Kat looked back at Violet, who had dozed off, then slid their cooler in between the front seats to get closer to the conversation. Derrick felt chills go up his spine as she gripped his forearm to pull herself closer to the front.

With their exit approaching, Derrick changed lanes and slowed down for the ramp. As they veered into their exit, the van began to slow, and another loud explosion sounded from the back rear of the van, causing everyone to jump and look at each other. Derrick fought the van to the side of the exit and put it in park once they were at a stop.

With no one speaking, Derrick turned to find Violet sitting taller than everyone else with a big smile on her face. Shaking his head, he said, "You guys stay in here, I'll go check." Derrick replied. But before he could reach the rear of the van he was greeted with Karl, Jack, Gerald, and Simon to inspect the flat left rear tire.

"Damn!" Jack replied.

"We'll never hear the end of this," Karl observed, taking a deep breath.

"Maybe she's onto something?" Simon questioned. The other four men gave him a dirty look.

"Well, luckily we're not 200 yards from that service station. Let's get in and drive it there," Derrick instructed.

From inside the van came Violet's protest. "Drive! On a flat! Let me out!" Violet pushed her way through the side door. "You guys are going to kill us all! I'll walk!" Before they could stop her, she marched off toward the service station.

Derrick glanced back in the van, where Betty and June were giggling and Kat had her hand covering her mouth. With her eyes squinted, he knew she was laughing at them too. The men climbed back in the van and slowly drove to the service station.

"There's an ice cream shop across the street. Why don't we head there while you guys get the tire fixed?" Kat suggested.

Derrick raised an eyebrow. "You getting out of fixing the tire?" He smiled.

"Maybe," she replied in a flirtatious voice.

Derrick walked into the station. "Heard you had a balancing problem?" a man with overalls asked, wiping his hand with a greasy rag.

Looking around the shop, Derrick asked, "Did she leave?"

"Yep. Yelled something about everyone trying to kill her and then walked over to Bud's Ice Cream Shop." He pointed across the street.

"OK. Do you have a tire that will fit? I'll need a spare, too."

"I believe we can fix you up. An out-of-balance tire made it blow out?" he asked, still confused.

"No, the van was unbalanced with passengers."

The man cocked his head. "Unbalanced? Were you all sitting on one side?" He looked out at the van.

"I can go get her to explain," Derrick smiled with a thumb over his shoulder pointing to the ice cream shop.

The mechanic shook his head. "No, I'll take your word. Give me about 30 minutes."

Chapter 16

During the quiet ride from Bud's Ice Cream shop to the hotel, Kat gathered her files for the rooms. Dishing out keys, she commented to Jack and Gerald, "Looks like you two and I have single rooms." She handed the key card to Jack, who paused staring at the card.

Turning to Gerald, he said, "I don't have to have my own room; you want to bunk together?"

"Only if there are two queen-sized beds," Gerald replied.

Handing the key back to Kat, Jack went on, "You're taking all the fun of bunking together." He laughed. "Save the money—we'll stay together,"

She smiled and walked back to the front counter. Derrick and Simon brought in the last load of luggage from the van and set it in the lobby. One by one, everyone retrieved their bags and headed to their room. Kat handed Simon and Derrick their room key, "They only had a king left. Hope you two don't mind sleeping together." She spun toward her bag. Without untracking, the two young men stared at their key cards. "I'm joking," she added, flipping her hair out of her face.

"OK, I'll admit you had me there for a second," Derrick replied.

Simon shot him a funny look. "What? My physique isn't good enough?" He grinned.

"Nope." Derrick followed Kat to the elevator.

Stepping off at their floor, they found Karl and Betty arguing in the hallway about their lost key card. "Karl, there should have been two cards in the envelope unless you have lost one," Kat interrupted their discussion.

Karl pulled out the envelope, and two key cards fell out. Betty gave him an annoyed stare. Derrick unlocked his door next door to Kat's. "You want to meet downstairs in 30 minutes to go over tomorrow's schedule before supper?" he asked.

"Sure." She smiled and disappeared into her room.

Derrick and Simon walked in to be greeted by one king-sized bed, "Dude, she wasn't joking." Simon dropped his bag.

"I'll get it changed," Derrick said as he walked back out toward the front desk.

After changing rooms and getting settled, Derrick walked back downstairs without Simon to meet Kat. Choosing the stairs, he exited onto the first floor in the hotel bar beside the elevators. Jack was sitting at the old mahogany bar engaged in a conversation with the young female bartender. "How about a drink for our fearless leader?" Jack welcomed him.

"Maybe in a few. I need to meet with Kat first."

Sipping his bourbon and nodding, Jack said, "That would definitely trump a drink with me."

"It's not like that. We're meeting about tomorrow's schedule."

Saluting him with his drink, Jack went on, "And that is where it all starts."

Derrick tried to ignore the comment, but contemplated if this was a start. *If the Cedar Branch is closing, what would it matter if I asked Kat out?* He thought. Catching the elevator doors opening in the corner of his eyes, he watch Kat stroll into the foyer, looking his direction. Her smile crippled his heart and caused him to inhale another breath. She had changed into a pair of lite blue shorts and casual top, Jack reached from his bar stool and drew her in for a one-arm hug as she walked by. Derrick watched as Jack whispered in her ear.

She playfully pushed off him and walked up to Derrick. "Someone has already started this evening," Derrick nodded toward Jack.

"Something tells me this might be his ritual," she answered. Derrick started to ask what Jack had whispered, but was cut off. "So what did you think about today?" Kat was asking with a smile.

"Two flat tires in one day? I hope it gets better," Derrick said.

"Minor setback. I think it went well, except the musical."

"It was fine."

"Where is Simon?" Kat looked around.

"I think he's coming," Derrick answered, looking back at the bar where the bartender was laughing at something Jack had said.

"We definitely have a crew of characters." She nodded toward Jack. Derrick answered with a smile. "What do you think his real story is?"

"Real?"

"Yea. He turned down a single room and asked Gerald to room with him."

"I don't know. A socialite?"

"No, there's more to it." She focused back on Derrick. "So, tomorrow?"

The two of them sank into the schedule for the following day with Derrick drifting back to his previous thought about the policy that kept employees from dating. The lobby and hotel bar gradually transformed into a social forum, with travelers resting their feet and relaxing with drinks.

"You want a drink?" Derrick interrupted Kat.

The question threw her off from discussing the schedule, "Well, I guess?" She reluctantly answered.

Derrick stood, asking, "What would you like?"

"Glass of red wine?" she answered, questioning whether she should drink while leading a trip or drink with a male co-worker.

Derrick leaned on the bar. "Two glasses of red. House is fine."

Jack shifted on his stool and faced Derrick. "When are you going to let this façade down?" He waved his hand in front of Derrick.

"Façade?"

"You like her, don't you?"

"Kat is just a friend and co-worker."

Jack placed his hand on Derrick's shoulder. "Whatever you and I talk about will always stay between us."

Letting his guard down, Derrick added, "She is beautiful."

The bartender set the two glasses of wine on the bar. "That's $9.56."

"I've got that," Jack replied to the bartender. "You better get back before someone pushes their way in," Jack said, looking back at another man who was talking to Kat. Derrick thanked him for the drinks and walked back.

"Here you go," he handed her a glass and shot the guy a look.

"Enjoy your trip and safe travels," the man smiled and walked back to his party.

"Complements of Jack." Derrick held his glass to a toast. She smiled and held her glass toward Jack, who smiled with a matchmaker's grin.

"So, a boat tour and wine distillery all in one day with this group. Should be an interesting day tomorrow," Kat commented, closing her folder with the schedules.

"I'd say so." Derrick took a sip of his wine, glancing at Kat through the glass.

Chapter 17

Betty and Karl exited the elevator to a rambunctious lobby of music, drinks, and people. Fighting their way through the crowd to the restaurant, Betty kindly nodded to the generosity of a group of men that parted the way for them. Karl grumbled under his breath about the social vibe of the lobby and followed Betty with a smoldering expression.

Kat stood to greet them as they reached the table. "Good evening, I was about to come check on you guys," she commented, pulling out Betty's chair.

"Oh, I'm sorry we're late." She smiled at the table. "Funny, it takes me longer to get ready only to look half as good as I used to."

"I think you look beautiful," Kat smiled.

"We'd probably been here quicker if we hadn't stayed in the party hotel," Karl snapped, looking back at the crowd.

"I'm sure things will settle down once everyone goes to dinner," Derrick answered.

Jack and Gerald were engaged in a conversation about New York while everyone else studied their menus. Part of the crowd began filing out the front door heading to other restaurants while a large group made it to the hotel restaurant, where they were sitting in small groups at tables.

Simon scanned the room, then leaned into Derrick. "Hey, you noticed that all the tables here are either a group of women or men?"

Derrick looked over the restaurant, replying only, "And your point?"

Simon raised one eyebrow and pointed to a table. "Does that guy's shirt mean anything to you?"

Derrick looked at the young man's rainbow colored shirt and started to say something when it hit him. They were in the middle of a gay convention. He looked at Kat, who was nodding her head not to say anything. He laughed at the thought of what Karl would say if he were clued in. Looking back at Simon, he smiled and shrugged his shoulders, "They'll probably never notice."

Jack stole everyone's attention as he raised a glass of water. "Here's to today. Derrick, Kat, and Simon, you guys are doing a great job with our trip." Glasses clanked over the table as they saluted their trip leaders.

"What is on the list for tomorrow?" June asked.

"Well, after breakfast and before it gets too hot, we are going on a swamp boat tour. We are eating lunch at a plantation and then visiting a wine distillery," Kat proudly replied.

"Are you a wine drinker?" Jack asked Gerald, who was reaching down to pick up his napkin.

"Not really, but I'm willing to try some," Betty answered, thinking he was talking to her.

"You don't drink," Karl answered. "Plus he was talking to Gerald."

"I might try a glass," she smiled.

The waitress returned to the table to take their orders, and before she could ask, Violet handed her the glass of ice water sitting in front of her, saying, "Can I get a glass of just tap water, no ice?"

"Yes ma'am." She took the glass. "Can I take everyone's order?"

Immediately everyone picked up their menus and began studying again. The waitress looked over the table, and with no-one looking at her, said "I'll go refill this and be right back."

"Don't refill it! Pour it out and put tap water in it," Violet demanded.

"Of course," the waitress said, leaving the table.

June, who was overwhelmed by the menu, asked everyone what they were ordering, but couldn't get an answer for the indecisive group. "I have made some tough decisions about acquisitions, trades, and real estate deals, but I have never had a tougher time deciding on what to order," Jack commented.

Pulling out a couple of packs of Splenda from her purse, Betty commented, "It takes us longer to decide what restaurant to go to than to eat."

The waitress returned with Violet's glass of water and placed it in front of her. Looking at the three cubes of ice floating in the water, Betty said, "I don't *want* ice." She handed it back. "Tap water." The young lady took the glass and disappeared through the kitchen doors. Within a couple of seconds, she reappeared with a glass of just water and a disgusted looked on her face.

"Are y'all ready?" she asked.

As everyone was ordering, Karl noticed the waitress wasn't writing anything down. "Don't you need to write it down?" he blurted out.

Smiling back, she replied, "No, I'm OK."

"You're supposed to be impressed that she can memorize our order," June said from across the table.

"I'd be more impressed if she wrote it down and brought it out correctly the first time!" Karl answered.

Betty put her hand on his leg. "It will be OK."

"If I order bruschetta for an appetizer, would some of you guys help me eat it?" Jack asked.

"I'll help," Gerald spoke up.

Jack nodded to the waitress, indicating the order as Betty spoke up. "I'll help too," she replied.

After the waitress left the table, Betty turned to Gerald. "How long have you been a widower?" she asked.

Before he could answer, Karl piped up with "Don't ask the man how long his has wife been dead!"

"It's OK," Gerald answered. "Doris passed away eight months ago."

Apologies came from the table. "How long were you married?" Betty asked.

"59 years," he smiled.

"That's beautiful," June replied.

"She was beautiful. We got to travel through the world and even walked across Spain." He took a sip of his water.

"The El Camino to San Diageo?" Jack asked.

"I see you know your pilgrimages."

"I do. I would have never picked you out to walk 500 miles."

"It was definitely out of my comfort zone, but I was in better shape back then and madly in love."

"You're a romantic!?!" June yelled. Everyone looked at her. "I'm sorry—I didn't mean to yell. I've been trying to figure you out this whole time, and it just dawned on me that you are a romantic."

"I don't consider myself a romantic; of course, I wouldn't any more even if I were one. Plus I think I'm easy to figure out."

"That is the typical answer I would expect a romantic to say. And not a person that romanticizes a woman—I'm talking about a man that sees the beauty and details in anything," June replied.

"You're not going to start talking about Mother Earth, are you?" Karl asked.

She just gave Karl a dirty look and then looked back at Gerald. "I'm sorry to interrupt your story; please continue."

Gerald spent the next few minutes talking about his marriage, kids, and life. His story was cut off by two men carrying trays to their table and the waitress placing everyone's meals in front of them—all correct, except for Karl's.

Chapter 18

After supper, the table slowly departed to their rooms or back in the lobby for drinks and small talk. Karl, being the last one to finish his supper, helped Betty out of her chair, then followed her to the elevator. Passing a small group of young men, he spotted one of them wearing a Navy shirt. "Are you Navy?" Karl asked, pointing to his shirt.

"No, sir, just a fan," the man replied.

"I served with the Navy for close to 15 years," Karl said, striking up a conversation.

"Thank you for your service," another man who was also wearing a rainbow-colored shirt replied.

"You're welcome." Karl looked at his shirt. "Unique choice of a shirt," Karl commented, clueless that the shirt was a national symbol for Gay Pride.

"Thanks," the man answered, knowing he didn't understand the shirt, but staying respectful to Karl and welcoming him into their conversation. Betty walked a few feet before realizing she had lost him to the group of young men, so she made her way to the bar next to Gerald and Jack.

"I see you lost your date," Jack grinned, sitting back in his bar stool.

"If he's going to be social, I'll let him." She glanced at Gerald's drink. "What is that?"

"Ice tea," he smiled.

The female bartender walked up with a towel draped over her shoulder. "I'll have one of those," Betty said, pulling her Splenda out of her purse.

"Yes, ma'am. One Long Island Ice Tea coming up." She pulled a glass down from the overhead rack and began mixing Betty's drink. She watched as the small group of men and Karl laughed about something. Her drink appeared in front of her.

"Thank you," she smiled, tearing open the two packets and pouring them into the drink, a drink she remained clueless about the liquor in. The bar tender looked on with a surprised look at her stirring in the Splenda. "Whoa! This tea is different," Betty replied with a sour-faced expression.

Kat leaned over to Derrick. "Should we get Karl before they tell them who they are? He'll likely stroke out if he finds out that he's in the middle of a gay pride convention."

"Nope—some things are best left alone," Derrick replied with a laugh. Simon excused himself from the table, leaving only Derrick and Kat, who continued watching Karl laughing and holding one of the guy's shoulders to keep his balance.

Back at the bar, Betty took another sip from her drink. "What makes this tea taste so different?" she asked the bar tender.

"I'm not sure. It's a typical recipe."

"Recipe?"

"Vodka, Gin, Rum, Tequila, Lemon juice, cola, triple sec, and syrup."

"Oh dear! I thought I was ordering ice tea." She looked at the glass that was already down 1/3 of the way.

"I'm sorry. I thought that's what you wanted. Here, let me change that." The bar tender snatched the glass.

"That's quite a bit different drink from ice tea," Jack replied.

"Yes, it is," Betty answered, widening her eyes and trying to stop the room from slowly turning.

Karl shook the hands of all the young men and made his way to the bar with a big smile. "That is a great group of young men," he said.

"Looked like you were have a good conversation," Betty replied.

"Good guys. They are from Atlanta, one of them is a lobbyist." He paused, then asked, "You OK?"

"Yes. Why?" Betty asked.

"You seem to be smiling funny."

"Take her to your room in the next 15 minutes and you might be smiling funny too," Jack said, talking into his glass.

"What's that?" Karl asked, not hearing him.

"Oh, nothing. Just answering Gerald's questions."

"I guess we better go," Betty said, trying to stand up from her bar stool. She slightly fell into Karl. "Whoa, sorry," she smiled.

Karl helped her to the elevator. "Are you sure you're OK?" he asked as they disappeared around the corner.

Gerald looked at Jack. "Two things could possibly happen there, and both of them lead to a lot of sleep."

"That's the funniest thing I've heard all day," Jack laughed, slapping Gerald on the back.

Derrick and Kat walked up to the bar. "Better pace yourself, gentlemen; it's a long week," Kat joked with them.

"Sweetheart, I've been pacing for 81 years. You start out in life not caring about the end, then you worry about the end, then you wonder if the end wants you!" Jack smiled.

"And my pacing is making sure there's a restroom within the proper distance," Gerald held up his unsweet ice tea.

"I'm gonna let you guys enjoy your time," Kat replied with her hand on Jack's back. Smiling at Derrick, she vanished through the door into the courtyard.

Jack looked at Derrick, who was standing in front of the bar. "Son, are you blind and dumb?"

"I'm sorry?" Derrick asked, confused.

"A pretty girl smiles at you and walks to the pool, and you just stand here with a dumbfound grin." Jack pointed to the door. "Matter of fact, don't answer the question." Jack climbed off his bar stool and shoved Derrick toward the automatic sliding doors leading to the outside pool.

Popping out of the doors as though pushed, Derrick spotted Kat settling into a chair with her phone in hand. The light glistened off her cheeks and highlighted her eyes, but kept her from noticing Derrick walking up. *What am I supposed to say? Hello Kat? Whatcha doing? Do you have a minute? Minute? For what? Damn it!*

"Hey! You startled me," Kat said, looking over her phone. Derrick stood paralyzed like a middle school boy at his first dance. "Did you need something?" she asked, smiling.

"No, I was just walking through. Have a nice evening," he said, walking past her toward another set of doors.

She watched him walk through the doors, thinking *I wish you would have stayed.*

As the evening grew into the night, the hotel bar slowly emptied, with travelers turning in from a long day. Gerald tipped the bar tender, saluted Jack, and made his way to the room. With the music of Harry Connick, Jr. playing in the background, Jack sat at the bar alone, stirring his drink with a plastic straw. "Everyone left you?" the bar tender asked.

"Yep, they're strong out of the gates, but not much for stamina."

She hung a few glasses after drying them, "You want one for the road? Time to close."

"Nah, I was told I need to pace myself." He smiled and walked to the elevators.

Chapter 19

With light coming through the curtains that were cracked open, Gerald stretched his arms and sat up to the aroma of coffee. "Did you sleep?" he asked Jack, who was quietly sitting at the table with a paper in hand.

"Slept great. Coffee?" Jack asked.

"I'll wait till breakfast." Gerald stepped into his slippers and walked to the bathroom. Jack flipped to the cartoon section of the morning paper after opening the curtains to allow more light. He laughed out loud at a comic strip, thinking about his night of sleep, the first time he had slept all night in a long time.

"So, you ready for this boat tour this morning?" he yelled at Gerald with the bathroom door still closed.

"Sounds like fun," Gerald replied. Jack laughed again at another strip. "What's funny?" Gerald added as the door opened.

"Just the funnies. And the thought that half our group could make a great comic strip."

"Ha, I'll agree with that."

Everyone was congregating in the hotel restaurant for breakfast, so Jack and Gerald walked down together to find June and Violet already sitting at the table. "Good morning, gentlemen," June smiled.

"There's a nice buffet here," Kat added. "We figured everyone could eat on their own time." She set her plate down.

Jack and Gerald joined Derrick and Simon at the buffet and filled their plates with sausage, bacon, and eggs. Once back at the table, Kat looked at their plates. "No fruit?" she asked.

Jack set his plate down, saying, "I've eaten bacon, smoked, drank, chased women, and been chased by women... and some angry boyfriends, and I'm still here. With my luck, I would eat fruit and contract some foreign parasite and die. Not the way I want to go out," he replied, smacking on a piece of bacon.

"Actually many fruits contain compounds that deter or kill parasites," Gerald spoke up.

"Gerald. You're killing my joke."

"Oh, sorry."

The elevator doors opened with Karl and Betty stepping off and slowly making their way to the table. Betty was wearing sunglasses, and Karl was wearing a disgusted expression. "You think he's mad?" Gerald asked.

Before Jack could answer, Kat greeted them with a "Good morning" and helped Betty to her chair.

"It's morning," Karl answered, looking at everyone's plate.

"Is the light bothering you?" Kat asked, clueless about the sunglasses.

"Everything is bothering her this morning," Karl grumbled. "You want me to fix you a plate?" he asked Betty.

"Please," she answered.

The waitress walked up and filled their glasses with water. "Would you like coffee?" she asked.

"Coffee for him and unsweet tea for me," Betty asked.

"Make sure it's only unsweet tea!" Karl yelled across the restaurant as he walked to the buffet.

Betty pulled out her Splenda and two trays of pill dispensers. Karl set their plates down and argued about pills for five minutes before eating. The conversation started about the day and the boat ride. June expressed her concerns about not being able to swim if the boat sank, and Derrick did his best to convince her that it wouldn't sink, but could not prevail against her stubbornness.

A phone at the table began to ring, and the only people who checked their phones were Derrick, Kat, and Simon. Kat looked at June. "Is that your phone?"

She shifted, pulling her phone out of her pocket. "I was wondering why my leg was vibrating. I thought it was going to sleep," she replied before answering the call. She placed her hand over the phone. "It's the police chief," she said to Violet.

"What does he want?" she asked.

"He wanted to have someone fix the floor so critters won't get in the house."

"OK," Violet answered.

"The police chief is your carpenter?" Jack asked.

"No, the floor in one of our rooms gave way." She didn't want to give too much information.

June hung up the phone. "It makes me nervous," she said. Violet gave her a dirty look. "Don't give me a dirty look." June went on. "They should know so when the police come arrest us, they'll have a clue." The table became dead silent, with everyone ready for the story.

"Don't worry about it. The less we say, the better we are," Violet snapped back.

June looked at everyone, and with a loud voice blurted, "We killed our attorney!"

Karl spit his toast onto his plate, coughing. "I told you they were crazy," he said out loud to Betty.

"Karl!" Betty snapped back at him.

"I'll agree with your husband," Violet answered. "We are crazy, but we didn't kill our attorney! At least not on purpose," Violet answered. The table stayed quiet and motionless.

"Maybe you should explain a little bit more," Jack said, picking up his coffee.

"Yes! Maybe you should," Karl added. Betty punched him under the table. "What?" He looked at her. "We could be next."

"OK!" June spoke up. "Here is what happened." And for the next twenty minutes, Violet and June explained the story and their fear of being guilty.

"If I had known that these trips were as good as this, I would have signed up to help a long time ago," Simon leaned over and whispered in Derrick's ear with excitement.

Derrick pushed him back. "I am sure that the police will understand. Maybe you should go explain your story?"

"We will. After we enjoy ourselves on this trip," Violet said, giving June a sharp stare.

"I think everything will be fine. Let's all meet back down here in 30 minutes to leave," Kat said, changing the subject.

"Sounds good to me," Jack said, standing. "And June, I wouldn't worry either. I've wanted to knock off my lawyer many times." He paused, "Now I know who to call." He smiled.

Everyone made their way to the elevator, with June and Violet stepping in first. Karl hesitated at the door. "Get in," Betty pulled him. With a disgusted expression, he entered and turned to face the door with his back toward Violet.

Joking, Violet whispered in Karl's ear, "Of course, killing has become fun. I wonder who we can kill next?"

With widened eyes, Karl didn't move.

Chapter 20

Swerving, Derrick tried looking at his cell phone map. "Let me read that?" Simon snatched the phone out of his hand. Caught up in a conversation about astronomy with Karl, everyone except Violet was clueless that they were lost until Kat asked out loud.

"No, just seeing some of the sights," Derrick grinned in the rear-view mirror.

"You've been lost ever since we left the hotel," Violet blurted out.

Simon pointed to a road as they flew by. "I think we need to turn down that one," he commented.

Before Derrick could hit the brakes, Gerald added from the back, "I'll bet there is another road that will connect. Take your next left, then go straight until you see another road to your left."

"Are you looking at a map?" Derrick asked.

"No."

Derrick was reluctant to follow his directions, but turned on his blinker to hang the next left. After taking a few left turns, the van came to a rest at a stop sign. "Turn right," Gerald directed from the back.

"You sure?"

"Yep."

Karl turned in his seat and looked back at Gerald. "Are you guessing? You've never been here."

"Just following the stars," Gerald replied with a smile.

The van took a right, and within a mile came to the entrance of the swamp boat tour parking lot. "Well, I'll be," Derrick commented. "Gerald, you might have to start riding up front as our navigator."

"If that happens, then Karl and Betty will need to trade seats with Jack, and he and Simon will sit in the front bench and June and I will swap seats," Violet said. Everyone remained quiet for a short second.

"I'll just stay back here," an answer came from the back seat.

Everyone climbed out of the van. "Good job," Karl said, placing his hand on Gerald's shoulder and then catching up with Betty, who was going to the restroom.

"There's a first," Gerald said to Jack.

"Nah, Old Karl is a good guy. Just takes him a while to warm up," Jack answered.

"Hope it doesn't take a week," Gerald said, walking toward the tour shack.

A man with a head full of red hair draped to his shoulders and a red beard to match met them at the dock. Karl stopped and gazed at his attire that consisted of a pair of blue jean cutoff shorts and a stained white t-shirt. "You work here?" Karl asked.

"Kinda—I own the place. Dennis, your guide, will be with you shortly. I'm guessing with all the youth here, you must be Cedar Branch."

"Yep, we're part of the football team." Jack smiled, leaning on the railing of the dock.

"I thought y'all looked in shape," the owner replied. In the distance, a humming noise grew louder as something approached from the trees. Within minutes, an airboat sailed around a grove of trees and blasted toward the dock. "Here comes Dennis now."

Karl looked at Betty, who had a grin on her face that stretched from corner to corner. Karl didn't have to read her mind: Riding in an airboat had been on her bucket list for years. The boat slid sideways to the dock, and Dennis stepped down from the seat to catch the pier with one foot. His appearance didn't stray far from the man who had greeted them with the exception that his white t-shirt spelled out the words *Big Cajun.*

"Bonjour!" The big man stepped onto the dock. Everyone remained silent, stunned at the 6'6" man that towered in front of them. "I see you meet da man." He pointed at the red-haired man that had greeted them.

"Dennis will take good care of you," the owner replied. "And he might come in handy with that football team." He smiled at Jack.

"He looks like he *ate* the football team," Jack replied.

"All right, skinny mullets first," Dennis said in a thick Cajun accent and grabbed Betty's arm.

"Don't call my wife a mullet!" Karl snapped.

"Na, na! It means thin person," Dennis defended his slang.

"Oh, that would be me," Betty smiled big and climbed in. One by one, everyone took their seats and strapped in—all but Violet, who was standing on the dock examining the boat.

"You hold my hand," Dennis coaxed her into the boat.

"This doesn't look right," she replied, looking at the seating arrangement.

"Well, damn!" Karl said from the center.

"What doesn't look right?" Dennis asked.

"We need to shift seating for the boat to balance."

"Ah! Madam, I promise nothing will tip dis here boat. I've done dis a long time, me."

She cocked her head and raised one eyebrow. "You single?" she asked, preparing to come back with a cynical remark.

"Ay," he answered, then leaned in to speak more quietly, "and if you leave your number, maybe we can go grab a bite later." He smiled.

A warm, flushed sensation sunk in with Violet, and with a glimmer in her eye, she stepped into the boat with the assistance of Big Cajun. "Huh, someone must have said the right thing," Jack observed.

Dennis fired up the big block Chevy engine and motored slowly to the channel. With everyone wearing headphones to protect their hearing, he yelled over the engine and propeller, "If you are ready, give me a thumbs up!"

Eight hands went up in the air with thumbs, and seconds later the front of the boat lifted out of the water with 550hp pushing them through the channel of cypress trees and cattails. They had a short trip to the marsh, where Dennis killed the engine and let the boat drift before climbing out of his perch and making his way to the front.

One by one, everyone took off their headphones, leaving their hair standing straight up as if they were still going. "Welcome to my home," Dennis started. "Today, I'll show you the life of da Louisiana swamp."

"Are you and the other guy the only guides?" Violet asked with a smile.

"Nah, I'm de only guide, he only owns the place. If y'all know your treasure hunters, then y'all would hear about him." He changed the subject and pointed over the marsh, "Ay, see that pop chock over dere!"

Everyone in the boat shift and looked. "What the hell is a pop chock?" Karl asked.

"Da little brown bird. Look past it and see the caimon?"

"What?" June asked.

"Caimon means *alligator* in Cajun French," Gerald replied from the back seat.

Karl turned to him, asking, "How do you know that?"

"Just picked it up in the past," he shyly answered.

"There are lots of gators here. We'll see many. Everyone OK with da boat?" He asked and received a nod from everyone.

"All right, we go." He jumped back up in his chair and fired the engine back up. As he twisted the throttle, the wind blew water 20 feet behind the boat, causing a group of cranes to take off.

Chapter 21

Coming around a bend in the dense marsh, the airboat slid like a rock skipping across the water, causing Kat to slide into Derrick. She tried pushing off with her left hand placed on his knee, but after another tight turn she found herself pinned against him. "Sorry," she innocently smiled. He gave only a smile back, worried he might stutter on his own words.

The boat throttled down and came to a gentle glide across a small bed of marsh grass with a grove of cypress trees in the distance. "Dis is one of the favorites for gators," Dennis said in his thick Cajun tongue. "Many *Poule D'eau* gather here, and it makes for good eatin'," he continued.

"What?" Karl asked.

"*Poule D'eau* is a small duck known as a coot," Gerald answered.

"Maybe you should interpret," Karl said.

Dennis made his way back to the front of the boat with a small ice chest, causing Violet to sit up straighter. Opening the lid, he pulled out raw pieces of chicken. "Dis here will bring up big uns." He pointed toward the cypress trees, adding, "Dere is a lot of *chaoci* here also."

Everyone in the boat turned to Gerald. "Raccoon," he gladly interpreted.

"Yea, de *vieux* knows his Cajun French," Dennis replied.

Again and as if at a tennis match following the ball, everyone turned to Gerald, "*Vieux* is old man," Gerald replied.

"Careful, Dennis, you're talking about our starting fullback," Jack replied. Dennis laughed in a deep tone.

"It's getting time to head in. I think we can go around dis here cannel and head toward da dock." Dennis pointed west.

"It might be quicker to back track and head that way," Gerald replied, pointing north.

Laughing, Dennis replied, "Thanks, but I been in dis marsh for long time."

He fired up the engines and proceeded in the direction he had pointed, only to find it led to a dead end in the grove of cypress trees. He killed the engine and asked Gerald, "Which way you pointed?" Everyone in the boat simultaneously pointed in the direction Gerald had showed. Within minutes, the swamp boat emerged from the marsh into the channel they had started in. "Well, I'll be dog," Dennis said to himself.

Drifting to the dock, Dennis hopped down and pushed off the weather beaten pier with his size 14 boot. "You folks keep ya seat until I get tied off." He turned to tie the boat. Once he turned around, everyone had already unloaded from the boat and were making their way to the one restroom. "Or not," Dennis said.

Derrick walked up to the line at the bathroom. "I believe I'll head to the back of the boat shop," he whispered to Simon and pointed to a dilapidated old building at the end of the parking lot. Stepping behind the building and unzipping, Jack, Gerald, Karl, and Simon followed suit.

Simon started laughing. "First one to finish wins?" he asked.

Jack, Gerald, and Karl looked down the line of men at him, "Son, you have no idea about an 80-year-old bladder. I'll be here half an hour," Jack said.

"It'll take me a half hour to get started," Gerald added.

"Will you guys shut-up? Trying to pee here," Karl said, staring at the sky.

Finishing and walking from behind the building, Derrick met Kat, who asked, "How's the men's bathroom?"

"I think we bonded in a weird peeing ritual."

She laughed. "Fun boat ride."

"Probably more fun for others," Derrick said, looking at Violet, who had Dennis cornered near the souvenir shop. Together they walked toward the couple to rescue Big Cajun.

"Thank you for the tour," Kat said, interrupting the couple's conversation.

"Where you folks eaten?"

"There is a place near the interstate we are going to stop."

"No, no. Best place to eat is Durbeau's. Dis here road will bring you to a stop sign, and Durbeau's is crisscrossed from de road."

"Sounds good. We'll have to take a vote," she smiled.

"I'll be right there," Violet said, hinting for the couple to give her and Big Cajun some more alone time. Kat giggled under her breath and pulled Derrick's arm as she turned to walk back to the van. Dennis watched with a distressed expression as the couple walked off.

After everyone loaded into the van, Violet, who was goggle eyed over Dennis, never noticed they had switched seats to play a joke on her. Halfway to the restaurant, Jack, who was in the passenger seat, turned to Violet, asking, "Did you get his number?"

She lifted her eyebrows, "Oh yea," still clueless to the seating arrangement.

"I believe I am ready for some homemade Cajun food," Karl said, climbing out of the van at Durbeau's.

"Honey, you know your ulcer can't handle spicy food," Betty replied.

"You only live once. Right, Jack?" Karl replied in an unusually good mood.

"Depends on what you eat. A bad ulcer can kill you many times."

Durbeau's had paid attention only to the Cajun food they served and not to the building that housed them. The screen door was held on by one hinge, and the siding on the building was splintered so badly that wasps had built nests in the cracks. When the door opened, the bell clanked with the clapper missing. "Are we sure about this?" Kat whispered to Derrick.

"Most mom and pop places like this are known for great food," Jack answered her.

"Your hearing is impeccable," she replied.

"What?" he asked.

"Your hearing—" She noticed him laughing. "Oh, haha."

When they were seated, an overweight lady brought out a handful of menus. "What y'all be having to drink?" she asked in a thick accent.

"Unsweet ice tea," Betty answered.

"Tap water with no ice," Violet answered, while the rest of the group ordered water with ice.

Studying the menus, Jack observed, "Back to the hardest decision of the day."

"Cajun food is not making it any easier," Kat replied.

The waitress returned with their drinks and a pad to write their orders down. "See, that's what impresses me," Karl commented, pointing to her notepad.

"Is the shrimp spicy?" Betty asked.

"Yes ma'am, but we can boil you some without de spice."

Closing her menu, Betty agreed. "That's what I'll have."

Derrick glanced at the bar that had a chalk board with daily specials written on it, but couldn't make out what the rest of it said. "What's the special?"

"Blackened red fish with sautéed crab meat and wild rice," the waitress answered.

Simultaneously, everyone shut their menus.

Chapter 22

Staggering out of the restaurant and holding their stomachs, the group slowly made it to the van. One by one, they climbed back into the van with expectations of napping on the way to their next stop. Violet missed her first step in the van and tried again, this time with help from June, who gave her a stern boost. Her foot slipped again, causing her to come crashing down to the ground. Everyone took a deep gasp as she disappeared from the doorway.

"June!" Violet shouted at her sister.

"I'm sorry, I was trying to help. Are you OK?" June asked.

Violet grabbed the side of the van to pull herself up as Simon hustled over to help her. As Violet rose, she screamed from a sharp pain running down her hip and leg. Kat and Derrick froze. "What is hurting?" Kat helped her back to the ground.

"I think my hip," She said with exasperation, then grabbed her arm. "And my wrist," she added.

Kat looked up at Derrick. "Let's give her a second to catch her breath," he said. The van began to empty with everyone standing near.

"Why did you push me?" Violet looked at June.

"I wasn't pushing you, I was just helping."

Violet gave her a sour look, "Thanks."

"Let's try to get up again," Derrick suggested, reaching around her to assist.

She let out another agonized sound. "I'm sorry. It hurts."

Kat pulled off Violet's shoe and felt for a pulse in her foot. Looking up at Derrick, she said, "She doesn't have a very good pulse." Derrick pulled his cell phone from his back pocket and walked off from the group.

"I bet if we go get Big Cajun, he'll help you get up," Jack replied, trying to ease the moment.

"If I wasn't hurting, I would say call him," Violet tried to smile.

Derrick returned. "Since you don't have a good pulse in your foot, I called for assistance."

"An ambulance?" Violet looked surprised.

"Yes."

"Oh, Lord, I don't need an ambulance."

"Sweetie, if you can't get up, we don't need to take a chance," Kat replied.

Karl leaned over to Betty. "Would it be rude if I went in and got a piece of the chocolate pie?" She shot him a look that didn't require an answer.

Seeing the commotion congregated around the van, one of the waitresses walked out, and in the distance a siren could be heard from the approaching ambulance. "That was fast," Jack commented, hearing the siren.

"There is an EMS station just down the street," the waitress explained.

"This is embarrassing," Violet said, looking down.

"Why don't you guys go back in for a minute? No sense we all stand outside in the heat," Kat said.

"Don't have to tell me twice." Karl turned and made a beeline to the door.

"Are you sure?" Betty asked.

"Yes, we might be a few minutes."

Everyone walked back into the restaurant, where Karl was already sitting and ordering his pie. Everyone ordered and sat back silently. Breaking the silence, Betty commented, "There were sure a lot of alligators out there. What did he call them again?"

"*Caimon*," Gerald replied.

"That reminds me of a story that happened at my friend's farm in southern Florida," Jack answered.

"What part? Naples?" Karl asked.

"No, this was near Okeechobee." Jack rubbed his chin. "I think it was '57 or '58. It doesn't matter—the late 50s. I had just went through my second divorce, and an old college buddy of mine lived on a farm with a few lakes on his property. I figured I would take off for a couple of weeks."

The waitress returned with waters for everyone. "Thank you," Betty smiled at her.

When everyone was giving their attention back to Jack and his story, he went on, saying, "My buddy had been having trouble with college kids drinking at one of his lakes and leaving trash. He could never catch them, so, since I was there for a couple of weeks, I told him we'd catch them.

One Saturday I drove down to the lake that he'd been having trouble at. I had a 55 Ford Falcon at the time."

"I had a 57 Ford Falcon," Karl blurted out.

"Red?" Jack asked.

"Two tone, red and white. I drove that car—"

"Get back to the story," Betty interrupted them.

"Sorry. Anyway, as I drove up, I noticed six to eight people swimming, and since it was private property, I figured this was the group my buddy had been trying to catch. I drove up fast so that they wouldn't have time to climb out of the water, and as I got close I saw they were all girls. College age. The next thing I noticed was all their clothes on a fallen tree trunk. When they saw me, they all congregated close to each other in the water. I stepped out of the car and walked up to the water. All of them wide-eyed and covering their chests. One of them yelled at me, "We don't care what you say, we're not getting out of the water with you here!""

The waitress returned with pie for everyone, and after serving, Jack returned to his story. "Anyway, after she yelled that to me, I thought for a moment of what to say. I didn't want to seem like a pervert, but they needed to leave too. So I walked back to my car and grabbed a five-gallon bucket from the truck that I stored my fishing gear in and said the first thing that came to my mind. 'I'm not here to look at you girls or ask you to leave... I'm here to feed my pet alligator.' And I held up my bucket."

Kat walked in to the laughter. "Sounds like I'm missing the party."

"How is Violet?" Betty asked.

"They are going to take her in to get her checked out. I'm sure she's fine." Derrick and June walked up behind Kat.

"Who went with Violet?" Betty asked.

"Simon."

"June, why didn't you go?"

"She still thinks I pushed her. Plus once she found out that Dennis was a volunteer EMT, she went quietly."

Jack gathered the checks on the table. "Only one thing left to do," he added.

"You don't have to pay for that," Karl said.

"My treat. Let's go taste some wine!"

As everyone walked to the van, Karl walked up behind Jack, saying, "I've heard that story before. In a joke form," he said quietly to Jack so no one would hear.

Jack smiled. "Some jokes are funnier told as a story," he said.

"I'll take that advice. Our secret." Karl pointed to both of them. Jack paused and watched Karl catch up to Betty, thinking this was a different side to Karl he hadn't seen.

Chapter 23

Receiving a text from Simon that they would be at the hospital for at least a couple of hours, Kat relayed the message to Derrick. The van was at its quietest with everyone passed out from lunch and dessert as they pulled down a gravel rock drive leading to the winery. Dust kicked up from the tires as it crawled down the windy road. "Not the most luxurious layout," Derrick observed, pulling up to the empty parking lot.

"It's not in the layout, it's in the bottles," a voice replied from the back.

Kat turned, "This is your forte, Jack." She smiled.

"Yes, it is," he smiled back.

While everyone was exiting the van, Kat's phone buzzed with a text. She remained motionless in the passenger seat, staring at the screen. Derrick walked around to her door. "Everything OK?" he asked.

"Yes," she lied, still looking at the screen. *How in the world did he get my number? This is the last person I want to hear from.* She sent a message: "How did you get this number?" She waited for a response that never returned.

"You coming?" Derrick yelled back to her as the group entered the winery that appeared to be no more than a wooden lodge. She tucked her phone in her back pocket and jogged up before the door shut.

Inside, the interior was much like one would think of a lodge—wooden floors with a thick layer of wax sending a reflection on everything that walked on it and the walls made with lapped cypress wood and lined with décor from Louisiana.

"Simon texted me and said everything was fine," Derrick looked at June. "They are going to release Violet soon. They think it was a pinched nerve in her back that has gone away, but she sprained her wrist," Derrick added.

"I'll never hear the end of it," she answered with a smile to thank him.

"I didn't think Louisiana would be a very good place to grow grapes," Betty said out loud, looking at a picture hanging from the wall.

"Actually, their grapes have been genetically modified to grow in the moist soil here. It's done in a lab in middle Tennessee," Gerald gracefully answered.

"How do you know that?" Karl asked. "You seem to be a walking encyclopedia," he said before Gerald could answer.

Gerald pointed to a laminated plaque under an artificial replica of a grape plant. "I just read it." Karl gave him a perplexed look.

"Well, hello y'all!" A lady appeared from behind the counter. Everyone's eyes grew as the obnoxiously loud lady greeted them. "Welcome! Y'all ready to start your tour?"

Betty looked up at Karl, who was standing behind her, and gave him the "Don't say anything" look. The lady waved them all through a door leading back to the warehouse.

Kat stopped shy of entering the door and looked at Derrick. "I'm going to run to the restroom first. I'll catch up," she said, not giving him a chance to answer. Looking back, she saw the door close to the warehouse and headed outside for a chance to call the number that had texted her.

Shaking, she waited for answer, "It's been a long time," said the voice on the other end.

"Monty! Why are you calling me? And how did you get this number?" She nervously quizzed him.

"I just called your work, and they happily gave me your number. So, you moved south? I've always wanted to see the gulf from Alabama." His voice had a creepy tone to it.

"I have a court order for you not to contact me! Much less stalk me."

"Orders are only meant to be broken. Where are you staying tonight? I was told that you were out on an orientation trip with a bunch of old people."

"Stay away from me! Do you hear me?" She screamed in the phone.

"See you soon, sweetie." The line went dead. Chills sprinted up her spine with the eerie remark from her ex-boyfriend and the emotions of a tormented hell exploded into uncontrollable tears. She felt her blood pressure rise and shook with fear of him finding her after all the measures she had taken to keep her identity hidden. Sitting down on a wooden pillion that roped off the parking lot, Kat wildly wept in terror of Monty finding her.

Inside, Gerald astonished everyone in the tour, including the tour guide, who actually asked him questions. "I thought this would be my field of expertise, but Gerald has truly impressed me," Jack said to Karl.

"He knows more than anyone I've ever met," Karl answered.

Betty and Derrick followed within hearing distance as she quizzed him about Kat, still trying to be a match maker. "I see how she looks at you," Betty said.

That caught his attention. "How does she look at me?"

"Interested."

"Stop playing Cupid," Karl said from a distance.

"Pretty awesome that you have been married for 52 years," Jack said to Karl.

Amazed that Jack remembered the number of years, "By the grace of God," Karl replied.

"Oh, I imagine it's more than that."

"No, actually only God could perform a miracle of keeping a woman around me for half a century. Believe it or not, I'm not the easiest to get along with."

"You're kidding me," Jack grinned.

"Ass," Karl threw a teasing elbow into Jack. The two of them walked the rest of the tour with everyone tasting wine but them. Karl questioned him about his business in New York and then his family. It was odd, Karl thought, that Jack was more talkative about his business than his family.

As the tour ended in the same place it started, Derrick wondered if Kat was OK, and walking outside, he found her sitting on the same pillion she fell to after her phone call. "You OK?" he asked, startling her.

"Yea. I just needed some fresh air. Too much spicy food," she answered, trying to hide her bloodshot eyes.

He started to say something about her eyes when a large truck pulled up in the parking lot with Simon hanging out the passenger window. "Figured we would catch you here," he yelled. Derrick watched the truck park, wondering why he was here and not with Violet, but his question was answered when he saw the back glass that had Big Cajun written on the back.

Dennis helped Violet out of the truck as the group gathered to witness her escort. "I figured it would be OK that I bring them here," he said.

"That's fine," Derrick said.

"You OK?" June said, consoling her and hoping she wasn't still mad.

With a big smile and doe eyes, "Yep," Violet answered.

Chapter 24

Kat remained quiet for the ride to the hotel, leaving Derrick to question what was really bothering her. The rest of the group filled Violet in on the tour of the winery that turned out to be eventless as Derrick and Kat expected. As the van pulled down South Pearl Street in Natchez, Mississippi, Derrick and Simon watched for the hotel that wasn't shown on their GPS. "Gerald, any clue?" Derrick asked.

"Isn't that it on the left?"

Derrick looked at Simon, who shrugged his shoulders. "I'd give him my seat if Violet wouldn't beat me."

"He's doing better in the back giving directions than you are from the front, no reason to tip the boat," Violet said, overhearing Simon.

"Tip the boat?" Simon mouthed the words to Derrick.

"Means, don't fix what's not broke!" Karl barked from behind him.

The van pulled in the drive of a locally owned hotel that

was inside an antebellum Victorian style house. The front porched wrapped around the corners of the structure with ornate white columns running from the ground to the roof line. The group slowly made their way to the back of the van to collect their bags and journey up to the hotel, noticing that it seemed overpowering for the small lot it sat on.

After receiving his room key from Kat, Jack asked, "How many beds in each room?"

"I believe two," she answered.

He turned to Gerald, "Want to room again?"

"Fine with me," Gerald answered.

Jack gave his key back to Kat. "We'll save some money again."

Overhearing them, the lady behind the counter piped up with "That room key goes to the most haunted hotel room in the South."

"If it makes noise, I'm not interested," Jack replied.

"No, she's quiet," the lady answered.

Jack grabbed the key from Kat's hand and gave her the one from Gerald's hand. "I've never had the opportunity to sweet talk a female ghost," he said with a smile.

Kat gave the key back to the lady without remarking on Jack's comment and picked up her bag and headed to her room. Derrick stopped her, asking "You OK? You don't seem yourself."

"Yeah, I'm fine. Lunch didn't agree with me," she lied.

Jack and Gerald met up with Karl and Betty in the hallway. "We would be staying on the second floor of a hotel with no elevators," Karl grumbled.

"We'll lead the way; got a date with a female ghost," Jack

replied, looking up the wide stairwell. Three minutes later, everyone had made the extensive climb and congregated in the hall with their rooms adjacent to each other. "That's going to be a tough climb after your Long Island Ice Tea tonight," Jack joked.

"Oh Lord, I won't make that mistake again," Betty laughed.

Jack and Gerald barely got their bags set down before Karl walked into their room. "Haunted, huh?" He examined the tall ceilings and antiqued wallpaper that was breaking loose from the top corners. A single lamp lit the room from a round table that didn't fit in the corner it was placed. "Tonight is supposed to be a good meteor shower if you gentlemen want to sit outside," he said.

"Is it going to be cold?" Gerald asked.

"Cool, not cold. Bring a jacket," Karl suggested and walked back to his room.

"Cold nights are the best to watch meteor showers, not sure why," Gerald said as he unpacked.

"You're not sure? That's a first."

A light knock sounded from their open door. "Supper in 30 minutes across the street at the restaurant. Take your time," Derrick announced. The two men waved to him, suggesting they would be there. Jack went through his ritual of unpacking and hanging his clothes in the closet; staying in hotels was nothing new for him. Often he would stay in hotels around New York for business instead of fighting traffic to get back to his apartment.

Gerald had disappeared into the bathroom and Jack was finishing hanging his shirts and pants in the closet when the room dimmed. Looking around the closet door at the room that was lit only by the remaining light coming through the window, he said, "That's strange" to himself. He walked to the lamp and tapped the bulb, thinking it had burned out, and from habit he pulled the cord and the lamp turned back on. Smiling, he said, "Well, hello, sweetheart" as he looked around the room.

"I don't mind rooming with you, but I draw the line at being called sweetheart," Gerald replied from behind him.

Laughing, Jack said, "I think our ghost just turned out the light."

"As long as she doesn't turn it on during the night, we'll get along just fine." Gerald put his tooth brush in his bag.

The group gathered in the lobby of the restaurant across the street waiting on their table and Karl and Betty. Violet looked at Derrick, asking "Where's our fearless female leader?"

"She isn't feeling well."

"She hasn't acted like she feels good. We'll check on her after supper," June replied.

The hostess showed them to their table and took their drink order. A few minutes later, a waiter returned with drinks and set a glass of ice water in front of Violet, who handed it back and again explained the no ice, tap water order. Returning with the correct glass, Jack asked him, "Is there anywhere to have a cocktail outside around here?"

"Yes sir, just a block down is a tavern with an outside courtyard."

Jack nodded to Karl. "There's our place."

"For?" Violet asked.

"Viewing a meteor shower," Jack answered.

"It's too cold for that."

"Cold weather doesn't hold moisture like summer nights. Makes it clear to see stars," Karl chimed in.

Jack looked at Gerald. "There's your answer."

Karl, hearing that, added, "Winter is also the best time to see constellations like Gemini, Orion the Hunter, and Monoceros."

"How do you know that?" June asked.

"Don't get him started," Betty replied, but too late. Karl sat up in his chair and during supper, gave the group a crash course in astronomy.

After supper, the group made their way to the sidewalk and started across the street. "You're not coming to the courtyard?" Karl asked Betty, who was following the Stevens sisters.

"No, I'm tired," she answered.

Karl looked at Gerald and Jack, who started toward the tavern, and then followed Betty across the street. "What are you doing? Go with the guys," she said.

"You sure?"

"Yes," she smiled and turned him toward the two men walking down the street. He jogged across the street to Jack and Gerald, who weren't aware he wasn't already following them. They ordered drinks and walked out into the dark courtyard for the meteor show. From their chairs, they could see the upstairs of the hotel and their room.

"Did we leave the light on?" Gerald asked, pointing to their room. Karl and Jack looked up in time to see the bedroom light go off and then seconds later turn back on. For the next hour, they watched the bedroom light, missing the extravagant show in the sky.

Chapter 25

"Kat, I'm sorry. He told me he was calling about your parents, and to be honest I believed him," the Cedar Branch director told her.

"He's good at convincing," she replied.

"Do you think you are in danger? If so, we need to pull you from the trip."

"No, I don't."

"Are you sure? We don't need to put our retirees at jeopardy."

"Yes, if I was I would leave," Kat answered, rubbing her forehead.

"Well, get some sleep, and I'll check back in with you tomorrow."

"Thanks." Kat ended the call. Monty had shown a tendency toward violence with her, but hadn't laid a hand on her, not that she ever gave him a choice. She lay back on the bed that hadn't been turned down yet and took a deep breath. *Everything is going to be OK—he won't come around while I'm on this trip,* she thought. A forceful knock came from the door, and Kat sat straight up with her heart pounding.

As she tip-toed to the door another knock came, this time lighter and less intensive. "Who is it?" she reluctantly asked.

"It's Derrick." She felt an overwhelming sense of relief flush through her body. Opening the door, he said, "Sorry, I didn't mean to knock so loud the first time. These doors are lighter than they seem." He demonstrated.

"It's OK. What's up?"

"You OK? Seems like you have more on your mind than just feeling bad," he asked.

Are you questioning me? And why the third degree? What am I thinking—it's Derrick. "Just a stressful matter at home. I'll be OK." She smiled with the thought of him truly asking.

Derrick started another question when the hall door leading to the stairs closed. He looked at Kat, then back at the door. "Wind, maybe?" he said.

"This place is supposed to be haunted," she laughed, but quickly stopped with a weird expression when a low moaning noise followed the closed door. "OK, maybe it *is* haunted," she added.

Derrick slowly walked toward the door with Kat following tucked safely behind him and looking around his arm. A distinctive scratching noise came from the door, and both of them paused in the hallway. Kat grabbed his arm. "OK, now I'm freaked!"

Feeling the warmth of her hand's death grip on his arm, he grinned and turned to her to say something, but before he could say anything, he saw her eyes grow wide with fear. Turning back, he saw the door slowly swing open. His heart started beating faster, but he wasn't going to let his macho be questioned, so with Kat pinned to his back, he slowly walked to the open door. Within feet from the doorway, a ghostly figure sprung into the doorway. "BOO!" Jack yelled.

Fear caused Kat's body to fill with adrenaline, and she pushed Derrick into Jack. He caught the elderly man from falling, and turning back to Kat, said "Really? You're going to sacrifice me to the spirits?" he laughed.

"Sorry," she innocently smiled with a grin full of teeth.

Karl and Gerald appeared laughing from the stairwell. "He got you guys good," Karl said.

The loud scream from Kat caused the hallway to fill with the rest of their group and a few others that were staying there. Apologizing to the crowd that filled the hallway, Kat punched Derrick in the arm and returned to her room, thinking *Why can't I find good guys like him?*

The following morning, everyone gathered downstairs for a continental breakfast and fresh coffee. Karl, Jack, and Gerald glanced at the pastries and wheat toast and as if speaking through telepathic waves, walked across the street for bacon, eggs, pancakes, and coffee that was strong enough to wake the dead. Simon joined without giving second thought to the hotel breakfast.

"How'd you guys sleep?" Simon asked.

"Better after taking care of the lamp!" Jack answered, taking a bite of eggs. Simon glanced back at the hotel and noticed the lamp outside of Jack and Gerald's window balancing on the pitched roof.

Derrick walked in, saying, "Figured I'd find you gentlemen here."

"Pull up a chair." Karl pointed to an empty table beside them.

"Kat sent me over to relay a message that we'll be checking out in 30 minutes," he said, sliding a chair in place.

"See! You're getting the hang of it," Jack said, pointing his fork at Derrick.

"Hang of what?"

"Letting the woman boss you around," he grinned.

"That'll never happen," Derrick answered, looking at the greasy menu. Jack, Karl, and Gerald stopped chewing their food and gave him a blank stare. "What?" Derrick asked, seeing their surprised look as if he announced kingship.

"You'll understand in fifty years," Karl answered, going back to his plate.

"Well, again there's nothing there with Kat." Derrick hated to mention there was ever a conversation with Simon sitting at the table.

"Son, are you blind?" Jack asked and laughed. "Did you see how she clinched onto you last night?"

"You scared her. Plus she quickly offered me to the ghost by pushing me into you."

"Mere teasing and playing hard to get," Jack answered.

"I don't think so," Derrick looked at Simon. "They are trying to fix up Kat and me."

"I can see you two together; she acts different with you around," Simon answered with a mouth full of bacon and in a demeanor that said he didn't care either way.

Derrick spotted Kat crossing the street and making her way to the restaurant, her hair flipping back and forth bringing him back in the trance. As if in slow motion, she opened the door and smiled as if she never had a bad day. "Good morning, pastries and rolls not good enough for you?" she joked with the men.

"Foo-foo food. Real men eat greasy food," Karl answered.

She turned to Derrick, who was still in a dream. "You ready to pack the van?"

"What?" he snapped out.

"We can't be late for the riverboat cruise," she replied, unaware of his hypnotic trance.

"Yea, I'll be right there."

"OK. Bye, gentlemen," she flirted.

Derrick turned back to the table that was focused on him. "You are so blind! Go! We'll get your tab," Jack waved him on with his hand.

Chapter 26

Even with a short drive to the river, Violet wouldn't get in the van until Karl got back in the front with Betty. "Will you get up here?" Betty coached him.

"I don't see why in the hell it matters where we sit! This isn't a boat, it's not going to tump over!" Karl answered, squeezing to the front of the van. Violet stood quietly in the doorway of the van waiting on him to get to his seat.

Sitting beside June, Violet insisted, "That makes sense. We need to make sure that everyone sits in the proper place on the riverboat so it won't tump over" A loud sigh fell over the group with the thought of Violet controlling the riverboat. "I'm just kidding, everyone knows that boats are balanced for weight," she said out loud.

"Then why in the—" Karl was interrupted with a jab to the ribs from Betty.

Derrick put the van in park and turned in his seat. "Does anyone need to grab a jacket? It can get cool on the river." Everyone met him at the back of the van to claim their jacket, which meant taking out the luggage and repacking. Violet stood over the bags as Simon reloaded the van, overseeing that he did it correctly, and after a few remarks about him trying to make shortcuts, they were able to catch up with the rest of the group that was loading the riverboat.

Kat stood at the end of the ramp with their tickets. After Violet took her ticket and walked onto the boat, Simon took his ticket, grumbling "How many times am I going to have to reload the van?"

"It's their trip, not ours," Kat replied, trying to make light of the complaint.

"She's going to find herself swimming to shore," Simon fussed under his breath, noticing a grey Civic with a young guy wearing rimmed-glasses watching them. *That's weird*, he thought.

As the boat shoved off, Jack held onto his hat with the river wind blowing through the decks of the paddleboat. Steam poured out of the stacks with the engines cranking at 100% and the 80-year-old vessel pushing upstream. Betty and Karl leaned over the railing watching their dock appear smaller and smaller, reminiscing about a similar trip they had taken 30 years earlier. "Why is it that I can remember everything about that trip, but I can't remember what I had for breakfast?" Betty asked.

"Because I wasn't at breakfast, and you didn't have anything good looking like me to look at," he joked.

"That can't be it," she grinned at him, then snuggled against his arm, feeling the warmth that she had experienced for half a century.

The Stevens sisters sat on a bench on the front of the boat with the wind blowing their hair back. "What do they call the front of the boat?" June asked Violet.

"The front!"

"No, is it the stern or port?"

Violet gave her a funny look. "It's called the forward! As in going forward." June smiled, shook her head, and tucked her arm under Violet's arm. Together the sisters sat and watched the bends of the river pass with every turn. With years quickly ticking away, the two of them seemed to forgive faster and savor the moments. Habits that used to make each other cringe had turned into appreciations. June was noticing Violet's memory levels slipping, and a mother instinct she never realized she possessed had begun to take over, a secret reason why June pushed for them to move to Cedar Branch.

Gerald had snuggled down in a seat with his Members Only jacket giving him warmth and dozed off, leaving Jack by himself on the port side. He gazed out at the riverbanks and the wildlife that littered the shore. For the first time on the trip, he found himself alone, a state he fought against. Now without his assistant, whom he paid more for the company than for the need of someone helping him, his gut was tied in a knot with the lonely feeling.

Karl kissed the top of Betty's head and pulled her tight, noticing Jack standing alone. "Do you mind if we go stand next to him?" Karl asked. Betty cocked her head, seeing a different side to him; he hadn't been someone to take to people he didn't know well.

"Go ahead—I'm going to step into the ladies' room," she smiled.

"I bet the catfishing is good here," Karl said, walking up to Jack.

With a surprised look and smile, Jack answered, "I remember catching channel cats growing up on my grandfather's farm."

"Running trot lines?" Karl quizzed.

"Yo-yo's. We'd stay up all night with a Q-Beam flashlight and a stolen cigar from my grandfather's stash."

"Good times," Karl said, looking out over the water, "We get back from this trip, I say we go yo-yoing."

"You have a place?" Jack perked up with the thought of reliving his childhood.

"I'm sure we can find a place." Karl looked at Gerald, whose arms were folded and head slumped over. "You think he's sleeping?"

"Hope so," Jack laughed. "We need to take him to the store and replace those Velcro tennis shoes."

"Why so?"

"It's a sign that you're letting old age catch you," Jack replied.

Derrick and Simon walked up. "You guys saving the world?" Derrick asked, smiling.

Jack pointed to Gerald. "One old geezer at a time." They laughed. "Where's your girlfriend?" he asked Derrick.

"Kat is talking with Betty inside at the bar."

"Bar?" Jack looked over Derrick's shoulder in the glass door. "Might have to check this out." He led the group inside to the two ladies that were sitting on bar stools, Betty drinking her normal ice tea with two empty Splenda packages crumpled on the bar.

"It was too cold out there for me," Betty smiled.

"A good Long Island Ice Tea will warm you up," Jack grinned.

"Ha, I learned my lesson," she replied.

"Maybe we should go ask them if they would like to join us," Kat replied, looking through a glass window at the two

Stevens sisters sitting on a bench in the front of the boat.

"They'll come in if they want to," Karl replied and ordered a coke.

As the seventy-eight foot vessel steamed north, the intercom echoed with the captain's voice giving the history of the ship, river, and life in the 1800s on the Mississippi River. The group sat quietly at the bar and on the front deck, listening to the history lesson. Gerald never moved, drifting away in a sweet dream about earlier life and the beauty of his wife. As he slept, a single tear fell from his cheek.

Chapter 27

As the Queen of the Mississippi turned toward the port-side, catching the current and heading home, Derrick walked out to check on the Stevens sisters, unaware of being followed by Kat. Walking around the corner, he found June resting her head on Violet's shoulder, her long grey hair flapping in the wind. "You two doing OK?" he asked.

"Never been better," Violet answered.

June sat up straight and smiled. "I didn't mean to wake you," Derrick said.

"I wasn't asleep," June said, looking behind him. "How are you doing?" she asked Kat.

Derrick started to answer, thinking she was talking to him, but refrained when he heard Kat reply "Fine."

"What is everyone doing?" Violet craned up to see some of the group sitting at the bar.

"Getting hungry, I think. We'll be back at the dock before long and head for lunch," Derrick said.

"June, come with me to get a water," Violet ordered. "We'll be right back."

"I'll walk with you," Kat said.

"No, no. I want to talk with you guys. We'll be right back." She grabbed June's arm and dragged her inside before she could say anything. The steam boat picked up speed in the current and raced to the dock. Kat walked to the railing, glancing out over the muddy river and watched a white crane glide over the bank in search of its next meal.

Derrick, not knowing whether to sit and wait on the sisters or join Kat, walked over and leaned over the railing with his hands together and fingers locked. "First time on the river?" he asked.

"No, my father brought me out once in a small fishing boat. What about you?"

"I've been out here a few times," he answered, thinking of the many times he fished the river.

For the first time together, both of them had run out of things to talk about, but after a long awkward pause, Kat asked, "Where is Simon?" She looked through the window, then down the side of the boat.

"I don't know," Derrick answered, realizing he was missing. "He's probably sleeping somewhere."

A gust of wind pushed its way through, causing Kat's hair to flow behind her, and she brushed her fingers through her hair to keep it from tangling. Catching Derrick watching her, she gave a simple smile. *I hope she isn't thinking I'm some kind of creeper*, he thought.

"Tell me about your family," he said, fishing for conversation.

"Well, my parents live near Atlanta, and my sister is in

her final year at the University of Georgia."

"Nice, will you go back for the holidays?" he asked.

"Probably so." She thought about Monty finding her and putting a serious damper on her plans to go home. "Thanksgiving is a big deal to my dad, from hunting in the morning to cooking a turkey. He likes for everyone to be home." She looked up at him, adding, "And the parades."

"Yep, sounds like my family too. But they'll spend half the night deep frying a few turkeys and drinking too much beer."

"The good ole South—fry everything." She laughed.

"Boyfriend back at home?" he asked before he realized it came out. *Why in the hell did I just ask that?*

Wonder why he asked that? "Nope, the single life for me," she answered. "You?" *Why did I just ask that?*

"No, I stay so wrapped up in work so much there hasn't been a lot of social time," he answered.

"No social time for a social worker?" she grinned.

"Ha, I guess so."

She paused for a moment. "What will you do if Cedar Branch closes?"

"I don't know. To be honest, I haven't gotten that far yet. I guess start looking at other retirement homes. That will be tough; there's no place like Cedar Branch. What about you?"

"It still hasn't hit me yet. I love it down on the coast."

"Hopefully everything will work out," he said, seeing the dock come into view as they rounded a curve in the river. The large paddle wheel began slowing down, readying itself to reverse. "I guess they don't plan on coming back." He pointed at the sisters, who were sitting at the bar laughing at something Jack had said.

"Ha, I guess not." She started to walk in.

"Kat?"

She stopped and looked up at him, "Yes?"

He scrambled for something to say. "I'm sure everything will turn out fine."

"Thanks," she smiled, wanting to hear something else. What? She didn't know.

"I'll go find Simon." Derrick ducked his head and walked down the side of the boat.

She hesitated at the door, watching him walk away. *If this were just a better time*, she thought.

Derrick stopped by Gerald and gently shook him, letting him know that they were close to docking, then jogged down the wooden stairs leading to the first level. With only a few other people on the boat, he quickly made his way through the lower deck with no success. Running back up the stairs, skipping every other step, he made his way to the upper level, where he found a canopy and benches with Simon sleeping on one of the benches.

Derrick tapped him on the shoulder, "We are about to dock."

Stretching his eyes and still not awake, Simon mumbled, "Man, I'm sorry. I dozed off."

"No worries. Come join us in the galley so we can make a decision on where to eat lunch."

Rubbing his head, Simon said, "I'll be right there." As soon as Derrick disappeared back down the stairs, Simon stashed his pipe in his jacket pocket. *That was close.*

"OK, we have a few choices on where to eat," Derrick announced to the group. Jack and Karl sat back down at the bar. "You don't want to help?" Derrick asked them.

"You just asked the longest answered question." Karl huffed.

"OK." Derrick realized what he asked. "Burgers or meat and three?"

Karl and Jack stood up, "Burgers," Karl answered.

"But if there is a good meat and three," June said. Jack and Karl sat back down. Kat did her best to escort everyone off the boat and toward the van as the debate continued about whether burgers or meat and three. Fifteen minutes later, they pulled up to a pizza place.

Chapter 28

As the Van parked and everyone climbed out, Karl sat in place with his arms crossed, pouting about having to eat at the pizza place. "Oh, come on," Betty tugged at his arm. "I'm sure they have something you can eat."

"You can order hoagies or pasta," Kat assured him.

"Two things that come with cheese! As I said before, I'm lactose intolerant!" he barked from inside the van.

"*Intolerant* is the word I would use," Violet murmured under her breath.

"If you like, I will walk with you across the street to the burger joint," Gerald softly said in an empathetic voice.

"I don't need no damn sympathy!" Karl snapped and slid out of the van to follow the others. Betty smiled at Gerald and Kat in embarrassment and followed the rest of the group into the restaurant. The place looked as if it hadn't been updated since the 1980s, and pictures and local high school team memorabilia littered the walls with past championships and team colors. Jack stood in front of a baseball picture with a plaque below reading 1987 State Champions.

Karl looked over his shoulder. "They need to update their collection," he grumbled, still in a bad mood.

"They haven't won anything since then," a young waitress spoke up, overhearing his remark.

"They need to get a new coach, then!"

"No, they just need guys to work harder. Plus if they replace the coach, then I'll have to find a new job."

"What does working here have to do with a new coach?" Karl tested her.

"I'd have to move. My dad is the coach," she replied and walked to the table to take their drink orders.

Jack looked at Karl. "You might want to order a bottle of water," he grinned.

"Why?" Karl asked, confused.

"She might spit in your cola," he laughed and walked to the table.

After the young waitress returned with everyone's drink, including Karl's bottle of water, she convinced them about ordering three of the specials, pizza with the works including crawfish tails and shrimp. "What do you recommend for someone who can't eat cheese?" Karl grunted.

"You could get the Coaches Special without cheese," she answered. Everyone at the table started laughing. She blushed, explaining "I didn't mean that the way it sounded."

But to her surprise and everyone else's, Karl said, "I'll take that," closing his menu, defeated with the remark. She nervously took his menu, but quickly grew a smile when Karl grinned at her.

Four young men entered the restaurant and sat at a table across from the group. Jack noticed the young waitress's expression and sigh when they entered. "Do you have any more straws?" Kat asked.

"I'll get you one," the waitress answered, still watching the young men. As she walked past their table, one of them snatched her arm, causing her to stop. Jack, the only one at their table that noticed her uneasiness, watched her point her finger at one of the men.

June looked at Karl. "You know, they make a pill for lactose intolerant people."

Karl held up his pill box that Betty had set in front of him and shook it, "Does it look like I need another damn pill?" he grumbled. Everyone laughed.

The waitress set a straw in front of Kat. "What was that about?" Jack asked, pointing at the men.

"Just a bunch of rude guys that graduated from our rival school four years ago. You would think they would have grown up," she said.

The group watched as she walked past their table again, and one of them hollered at her, "Are you going to take our order or what?"

"Hey! Watch how you talk to ladies!" Karl yelled at the table.

The young men at first looked surprised, but one of them followed up with, "Shut up, old man!"

Karl gasped. "Old man?"

"Stay with the geriatric gang. You're out of your league here," the young man replied.

"I'm not sure who your father is, but he needs his ass kicked for not teaching you to respect others," Karl answered, feeling his blood pressure rise.

"My father is the largest construction owner around here. He taught me to take up for myself. You started this!" another young man answered.

The waitress butted in to take their order and tried to settle down the hostile environment. Karl overheard one of the young men tell her that the old people needed to mind their own business and then demanded another drink with more ice. Jack looked over the table at Karl and Simon, and as if they read his mind they all leaned in to hear his plan of teaching the group of young men respect.

"I wish we could slip them some laxatives," Betty insistently giggled.

"Do you have some?" Violet piped up.

"Please! We have more drugs than Walgreens," Karl blurted out.

Betty dug through her purse and pulled out a prescription bottle. Violet took the bottle and read it. "This would clean out a horse," she said with a laugh. "Here's what we do." Everyone leaned in closer. "You guys distract them, and we'll crush up two for each drink and stir it in when they're not looking."

"You sure you didn't kill your attorney on purpose?" Karl asked.

Violet gave him a sinister look. "Wouldn't you like to know?" Karl had trouble swallowing.

"We'll get them outside," Jack said and leaned back in his chair. "You two stay here. They'd be more likely to fight with someone close to their age," he said, looking at Derrick and Simon. Derrick was already rehearsing his statement to Cedar Branch and the local authorities about the killing of four young men.

Jack walked to the door, and looking back at the young men, asked, "Is that your truck?"

"Yea," one of them replied.

"I always wanted a big truck," Jack said and disappeared out the door, followed by Karl and Gerald.

"What are those old men doing?" the truck owner said out loud and followed them out with the three other men close behind. While they were outside arguing with Jack that they were not going to let him into their truck, Violet, June, and Betty slipped two crushed pills in each drink and got seated before the men returned. Derrick sat at the head of the table with his head buried in his hands as Kat watched, stunned by the group's revenge.

"I will never make any of you mad," Simon said as the ladies sat back down.

"That's a good idea," Violet replied, patting him on his back and grinning.

After everyone took their seats, the young men sat at their table, now trying to ignore the retirees. Violet winked at Jack, giving him the signal that everything was done. Jack turned in his seat. "I'll make a bet with you," he said to the young men.

"Not interested, old man!" one of them replied.

"You see, ole Gerald here is the guzzling champion from 1958. If he downs his soda before any of you can, you let me sit in your truck."

"And if we win?"

"I'll buy your lunch."

Two of the four men nodded their heads, "OK, you're on!"

Jack turned back to Gerald, saying "You're up." Then he lowered his voice, adding, "Make sure you lose."

"That won't be a problem." Gerald took his glass of cola and held it up. The four young men picked up their glasses and with the command from Jack, all five turned up their drinks. The four men downed their laxative-enhanced drinks.

"You should have retired in 1958," one of the men laughed. "Thanks for lunch, old man."

Jack smiled, "Yep! We lost."

Chapter 29

Everyone quickly scrambled out of the restaurant, leaving the young men to wonder why the fast exit. Betty took her time shaking her Splenda packets and preparing her to-go cup of tea and smiled at the waitress as she walked by the counter. "Take care," she said.

"Have a good day," the waitress said, almost in a complaining tone.

"Don't worry about them—they'll learn their lesson someday," Betty promised.

"One day," the waitress replied.

Walking out to the van, Betty found everyone loaded, with Karl standing outside the doors. "Will you come on," he hurried her.

"Oh, relax, the last thing they are going to do is chase us once those pills kick in," she smiled and stepped into the van with a cool demeanor.

Gravel sprayed the parking lot as Derrick floored the van, wanting as much room between the young men and themselves. With heads swaying back in forth in unison as the van took the next two corners, a soft giggling began stirring from June. Before long, the entire van broke out into hysterical laughter. "I bet those guys are fighting over the toilet right now!" June laughed out loud.

"Where to, boss?" Jack yelled from the back seat.

"Short ride to a place called Safari Gone Wild," Kat piped up, excited about the visit.

Puzzled, Jack looked at Gerald. "What gone wild?"

"Safari."

"I thought she said 'Sheryl gone wild.' I dated a Sheryl, and wild was putting it mildly," Jack replied, looking forward.

"Sounds like you should be the one in the zoo," Violet replied.

Leaning over the seat for only Violet to hear, Jack said, "Sweetheart, even a zoo couldn't handle this." Violet giggled under her breath as Gerald watched, clueless to what they were talking about.

With Derrick and Simon in the front and Kat sitting with Karl and Betty, the van was quiet, with only the sound of the blinker as they turned off the highway onto a gravel road leading to the drive-through Safari. A bright, colorful sign depicting animals appeared, pointing toward the entrance. The van glided into a parking space, and soon after the retirees poured out, heading to the restroom. "We'll meet at the front gate," Kat shouted, trying to catch everyone before disappearing into the restrooms. Jack gave a wave over his shoulder suggesting that he had heard her.

"I'm not sure what smells worst, the bathroom or the safari area," Karl commented, waving his hand in front of his nose. Betty rolled her eyes with the thoughts of his every morning bathroom ritual and the supply of scented candles that were never strong enough.

A bus painted black and white with Safari stripes and the top cut off pulled up in the parking lot. "We're going to ride in that?" Karl grumbled at Kat.

"It will be an experience," she replied.

"I'd rather have an experience in our van," he grumbled.

Gerald leaned over to Jack, saying, "Give Betty another Long Island Ice Tea, and he'll have an experience." The two men laughed.

"Good afternoon!" A young man greeted them stepping off the bus. "If you folks will start to load and find your seats, we'll start our tour." He smiled and stepped toward Kat, who was holding their tickets.

After everyone claimed their seats and settled in, Violet stepped on and examined the seating arrangement. "I guess that will do," she said and sat beside June.

The young tour guide looked at Derrick. "Don't ask," Derrick mouthed back to him.

He smiled, shut the double doors, and began to pull out. "Hold the bus!" a voice shouted from the back. The bus stopped, and the driver looked back at Jack. "Lost my phone," Jack said, and walked toward the door. "I laid it down in the bathroom," he explained, stepping off the bus. Moments later he returned, and again the driver began to pull out.

"Hold up!" June shouted.

"What now?" Karl crowed.

"I forgot my phone in the van," she said, stepping off the bus.

"What in the hell does everyone need with their phone on a Safari tour?" Karl snapped at Betty.

Patting him on his leg, she said, "Now, now. I'm sure they just want pictures." June climbed back on the bus, smiled, and took her seat. The driver looked at everyone to make sure there was no one else, released the brake, and started toward the fields.

"Wait a minute!" Kat shouted. The bus quickly stopped, bobbling everyone's head.

"Oh, for Pete's sake!" Karl barked out.

Kat smiled. "Just kidding. I figured everyone needed a laugh before we start."

"I'm sure we'll get plenty of laughs once we get in the park," Karl said, looking at Betty. She grinned and patted his leg again.

Simon turned to Derrick. "Who's Pete?" he asked, clueless.

Derrick shook his head. "You'll figure it out."

A voice came over the speaker system from the young driver. "Welcome to Louisiana's only drive-through Safari. We'll see animals from all over the world, with many of them hailing from Africa. I just ask if y'all will keep your arms and legs inside the bus; some of our friends have been known to bite."

"Kinda like you, Karl," Violet blurted over the group.

"Oh, ha-ha," he replied.

The convertible bus weaved its way through the 25-acre park with the young tour guide giving the history of the animals and the park. Joking remarks flooded the bus from all of the group about the different animals that were scattered throughout the park.

As the bus crossed over a cattle gap, Kat slid over to Derrick's seat, looking back at Violet, who gave her a frown at the sudden seat change. "I'll only be a minute," she smiled at Violet.

Frowning, Violet crossed her arms and snapped, "It'll only take a minute for this bus to tip over."

"Are the right side tires coming off the ground!?!" Jack shouted over the group. Out of reaction, Violet shot out of her seat and sat across the aisle from the side of the bus Kat came from, then looked back at Jack. "I'm only joking," he laughed.

Violet shot daggers through him with her brown eyes and slowly climbed back in her seat. Derrick and Kat looked at each other, astonished with Violet's peculiar quirk. Kat pulled out a file folder from her shoulder bag and started to ask Derrick about their drive to the hotel after the Safari. Unknowingly, she flipped her hair in his face, and the fragrance of her shampoo drowned out the foul aroma that had hit them the moment they pulled up to the Safari.

"You smell nice," he commented, then realized what he had said. Turning three shades of red, he tried to cover up. "I mean, your hair smells nice."

With a twinkle in her eye, Kat said, "Thank you," and smiled with little butterflies in her stomach. "Of course, anything smells better than this place," she played it off.

"No, your hair smells good," he said, letting his guard down.

Chapter 30

Pulling into the llama section of the park, the young guide announced, "I believe this morning our assistant vet accidentally released one of our crazy llamas."

Karl leaned over to Betty, saying, "As if most llamas are normal."

Jack yelled over the bus engine, "Are llamas from the US?" Then realized he was asking the wrong person. He turned to Gerald and waited for the answer.

Gerald cleared his throat. "Actually, the llama comes from South America. The Moche people used llamas as a burden animal and buried parts of the animal with important people as an offering to the afterlife."

"How do you know that?" Jack looked at him.

"And I thought llamas came from Spain," Karl added.

"No, the Spanish used llamas to bring down minerals from the mountains near Peru and Bolivia. One mountain in Potosi Bolivia had over three thousand llamas working before they brought in horses and mules to handle the work. Many of the Spaniards took the llamas back to their home country." He paused and looked at Jack, adding, "I guess I read it somewhere."

The driver of the bus ran off the road looking back at Gerald in the rearview mirror, astonished at his knowledge. "Sorry, folks, the gentlemen in the back is correct on where the llama hails from. I'm not sure about the rest," the driver replied.

"You can bet he's correct," Karl told the driver then looked at Betty. "I've got to pee."

"You're going to have to hold it," she answered.

"Like hell I'm going to hold it." He stood up and walked to the front of the bus. "Can you stop? I need to pee."

The driver looked puzzled. "There's no bathroom out here."

"I don't squat when I pee. Stop the bus!"

"Mister, I'm sorry."

"You're going to be if I don't step off of this bus."

The driver looked at Derrick for guidance. Rolling his eyes, Derrick replied, "You might as well stop."

"Mister, I wasn't kidding about one of the llamas getting lose this morning. He'll likely knock you down if he gets near you. He really is crazy," the driver tried to persuade him.

"Ain't no damn llama gonna mess with me," Karl grumbled, scanning the area. "Plus there isn't any nearby."

The driver stopped. "OK, but if you see a black and white llama running this way, you get back on the bus." He opened the door.

Karl stepped off the bus and looked up at half of the bus looking down on him. "How do you expect me to pee with an audience? Y'all move to the other side," he waved at them.

"Good Lord!" Violet shouted, with everyone shifting their seats.

Karl scooted close to the bus to give himself as much privacy as he could get and closed his eyes, concentrating on peeing. After a minute, he was about to relieve himself when a loud voice rained from above. "You done yet!?!" Violet shouted.

"Good Lord! Go away!" he shouted back.

Violet settled back in her seat. "I don't know what it is about men and shy bladder syndrome," she said to herself for others to hear.

"Or small bladders," June agreed with her.

"I don't know what old men you girls been hanging out with, but from experience, the older I get, the less shy everything gets," Jack replied.

"Amen," Gerald agreed. "Just takes longer."

"Maybe we should change the subject so Karl won't have so much pressure to use the bathroom," Kat said.

"He just needs to get rid of the pressure and get back on the bus! It's hot out here." Violet yelled over the side of the bus.

Karl shook his head. "I swear!" he said to himself.

"You done?" Violet questioned looking down on him.

Karl looked at the front of the bus, and since it wasn't a flat-front bus, no-one would be able to look down on him. He scurried to the front of the bus. "What are you doing?" Betty asked.

Karl shot her a dirty look. "If everyone would quit talking to me, we'd be leaving quicker."

As the group talked about bladders and Karl was concentrating on just going, nobody noticed the three llamas that walked up to see what Karl was doing. After a moment, Violet looked out at the front of the bus where only the back of Karl's head and three llamas standing behind him were visible. "If he knew he was being watched, we'd never get out of here," she said.

The three llamas watched with their ears pinned back and chewing on their cud. Gerald tapped Jack on the shoulder and pointed at the llamas. "They have the same expression as Karl does after taking his pills," the men laughed.

"Karl! You better get in," the driver shouted.

"I'll get in when I'm done," Karl grumbled to himself. He heard his name again, but continued to ignore everyone. Finally, after a miracle, Karl zipped his pants and turned to get back on the bus. Standing face to face with him and wearing a dumbfounded look, the escaped llama pinned his ears back and made a grunting sound. *Oh dear God!* Karl began to pray.

"Just ignore him and walk around him," the driver said.

Karl moved to the side, but the llama stepped with Karl, blocking his path and making another grunting sound. Karl struggled to swallow. "Remember, Karl, ain't no damn llama gonna mess with you!" Violet shouted with a big grin.

The llama took a step back and pawed viciously at the ground, making Karl think that he didn't quite finish peeing. The llama then reared up and just before he pawed toward Karl, a hand grabbed Karl's right arm and yanked him out of the way. Derrick pushed Karl on first, blocking the llama, and then stepped on the bus himself.

"Are you OK?" Betty asked, standing with the others.

"I'm fine! I told you no llama was going to mess with me," he played the incident off.

After he sat and everyone calmed down, the bus began to roll again with a shaken bus driver and eighty-one-year-old man. Karl looked over at Derrick and mouthed the words, *thank you.* Kat sat quietly in awe, thoughts of Derrick's heroic action rolling in her mind.

"Dang, Karl, that llama almost killed you," Jack shouted from the back.

"But you had him right where you wanted him, right?" Violet teased from behind him.

"No thanks to you," Karl said to Violet. "You'd let me die just like your attorney."

Everyone in the bus got quiet after the remark. Betty patted him on his leg. "Now, now, sweetheart, they're just picking at you."

Karl felt Violet's arms settle on his back rest. "Yea, Karl, we're just picking." She paused. "Plus you never know when you'll fall for one of my booby traps," she whispered in his ear.

Karl's eyes widened.

Chapter 31

Sitting around a table snacking on ice-cream and nachos, the group laid off teasing Karl for the moment and turned their attention to Derrick and Kat, who were leaning against a fence railing. Betty looked at June. "We need to get those two together; they would make a great couple."

"I don't think we have to work too hard at it," June replied, watching the young couple laugh about something Derrick had said.

The driver of the bus walked by and spoke to Derrick and Kat. "You two have your hands full," he observed, looking back at the cheerful group.

"It's not near what you think," Derrick replied with a laugh. "We just make sure they have rooms at night and meals during the day."

"If y'all are going to be here for a while, you should come check out the endangered bird sanctuary," the driver commented.

"Really?" Kat questioned.

"Yea, the park helps pay for the research that goes into the program and the releasing."

Kat looked up at Derrick. "Let's look. Simon can help anyone that needs anything." Derrick waved Simon over and told him that they would be only a few minutes and to stay close to the group.

The couple followed the driver, now a biologist. "How did you end up here?" Kat quizzed him.

"Once I finished my master's program in zoology, they had an opening and being so close to home, I jumped on the chance," he answered, holding open the door.

She looked at Derrick. "That's impressive," Kat commented, and walked in with Derrick trailing behind her. *I have my masters too.*

Simon pulled up a chair between Jack and Gerald, thinking it was the safest place to sit with this group and his nachos, but after setting his plate down on the table, both gentlemen snatched a chip. "What's New York like?" he asked Jack.

"Busy. But nice if you don't mind the fast-paced life," Jack answered.

"Were you married?" Simon asked.

Jack chuckled, "A few times." He looked up and noticed the entire group staring at him. "OK, five times. Couldn't find the right one." He looked back at Simon.

The group remained quiet except for Violet. "Go on, we're listening," she urged him.

"For what?" he laughed.

"Who were they?" June butted in.

Taking a deep breath and sitting back in his chair, Jack tried to respond. "Well, Delilah was the first girl I fell in love with. We were young and in college, and she had the prettiest blue eye's you have ever seen."

"What did you go to college for?" Karl blurted out.

"We don't care about what he went to college for," June interrupted.

"I don't really care about his love life either—it's none of our business," Karl snapped back.

Laughing, Jack answered both. "It's fine. And business."

"I think falling in love with her happened off the coast of Nantucket. Well, I know it did. We went to her folks' place for a summer trip, and she wanted to show me how to sail. Me personally... I just wanted to see her in a bikini." He elbowed Simon. "But as fate would have it, we were out in the ocean clipping along pretty well, and in the change of course the boom shifted across the boat, and well, I didn't see it. It felt like a truck had hit me and all I remembered was seeing the blue sky then darkness."

"Knocked you out?" Gerald leaned in for the story.

"Cold! But waking up with her light brown hair cascading around my face and her bright lips... Dang! Feels like yesterday." He looked at the table. "Fell in love!"

"Well? What happened?" Karl asked.

"Thought you didn't care about his love life?" Violet snickered.

"I don't. Wondering about the boat." Everyone at the table started laughing.

"You know, same old story. I fell in love with business and spent more time with my career than at home."

"Career or another woman?" Violet asked.

"Violet!" June exclaimed.

"It's OK. I will admit that I haven't always been the faithful one with my other wives, but Delilah was different. She was the one."

"What happened to her?" Betty asked.

"Fell in love with someone else. She's still in New York. I see her post things on line from time to time." Jack took a big swig of his water to help fight back the tears.

"Well, I still think we need to push a little." June pointed at Derrick and Kat walking out of the neighboring building. Their walk was slow with Derrick's hands in his pockets and Kat's stride unbalanced, as if they didn't want to out walk each other. As the retirees looked on, Kat laughed at something Derrick had said, unaware of their audience.

"You're gonna get them fired! Derrick told me that Cedar Branch has a strict policy about co-workers dating," Karl blurted out.

"Some things are worth getting fired for," Gerald spoke up.

Everyone at the table simultaneously turned to the elderly man, who had not said a word until now. He shrugged his shoulders. "I'm just saying."

"What were you guys doing?" Betty asked Derrick and Kat as they approached the table.

"You wouldn't believe it; they have an endangered bird sanctuary here. Over 24 different species," Kat replied.

"I'd believe it," Jack said, holding up a flyer on the sanctuary.

"You guys ready?" Derrick asked.

"Where to, boss?" Jack asked.

"Heading south to our next stop. We are staying in a historical inn that overlooks an inland bay," Kat broke in.

"Anything to do at this inn?" Karl asked.

"If we get there in time, there is a theater that is hosting a concert tonight, not sure what kind." She cut her eyes to Jack. "Or a swanky martini bar less than a block away."

A big smile formed on Jack's face. "I know where I'm going."

"The more important question is where are we eating?" Karl asked.

"There is a nice Italian restaurant attached to the inn."

"I don't eat cheese," Karl grumbled.

"You're eating nachos," Kat pointed at his empty plate.

"That's not cheese!"

"I'm sure we can find something for everyone," Derrick interrupted. Looking at Simon, he asked, "You and Violet want to get everyone in the van?"

With the van loaded, under the supervision of Violet, they pulled out onto the highway heading toward the inn. Derrick noticed a grey Civic pulling out behind him, but didn't think anything of it and with exhaustion setting in on everyone, the 45-minute trip was quiet and quick.

Chapter 32

"You guys want to wake up? We are here." Kat gently shook those in her reach. June stretched her arms above her head and nudged Violet to open her eyes. With half the van coming to life, Kat repeated in a soft voice, "Hey, guys, we are here."

Violet looked back at the two men who were still sleeping, Jack's head leaning back on the headrest and Gerald's chin tucked in his chest with arms folded. "We're here!" She shouted. Both heads popped up like they had been shot, and Violet smiled and turned to the door.

"And we wonder why she's never been married," Jack commented, blinking his eyes to adjust to the light that was left in the day.

Everyone congregated behind the van to collect their luggage and made their way to the entrance of the pre-World War II inn. Stepping next to Kat, Jack commented, "Just because we're old doesn't mean we want to stay in old places."

Smiling, Kat replied, "You'll enjoy the 5-star hotel we are staying in tomorrow night."

"Long as it has a bar, and that doesn't need to be a 5-star bar, just offer good bourbon," Karl responded, walking past her.

Gerald slowly made his way to the steps leading up to the doors. "Can I help you?" Kat asked.

"No, I'm good," he said in a soft tone.

"If you want a room to yourself, we can get you one."

"No, it's fine." He turned to her, explaining, "I don't think Jack likes to stay alone."

"Well, let me know if I can do anything."

"OK." He followed the group to the lobby.

Walking in the double French doors, the group found a lobby with marble floors and pristine furniture awaiting them. Gerald stopped to admire the chandelier that spanned half the ceiling with crystal pennants that hung in an orderly fashion. Karl and Betty set their luggage down, Karl immediately grumbling, "A swanky place like this doesn't have an elevator?"

"It's only two stories," Kat smiled.

"Only takes one step to break my back," he grunted under his breath.

Passing Jack, Kat repeated the offer she'd made to Gerald. "If you would like you own room I can get you one tonight."

He looked back at Gerald, who was still staring up at the enormous chandelier. "No, I don't think Gerald wants to be alone," he smiled. "I don't mind staying with him."

Tearing Kat's gaze away from Jack, Derrick picked up the sisters' luggage and proceeded to follow them up the stairs. Thoughts buzzed through her head as he joked with the ladies climbing the stairs, thoughts of a man who was not only patient, but compassionate. As the last one up the stairs, she checked to make sure everyone could get in their room before unlocking her door. After setting her bags on her bed, she turned to find her reflection staring back in the mirror. "He's perfect. Good looking, organized, and mature—something you haven't been perfect at finding," she said to herself out loud. "Come on, Kat, what's holding you back? You can't stay single forever."

"The right one is hard to find," a voice startled her from the doorway. Jack leaned on the doorframe, adding, "I should know."

"I'm sorry—I thought I had shut the door." She nervously reached for her file folder. "Is everything OK with your room?" She began blushing.

"Yep. This conversation will stay here," he assured her, "but you asked yourself the right question: What's holding you back?"

"Work." She wanted to drop the subject. Jack shook his head in acknowledgement and started to leave. "Was there something you needed?" she asked.

"What time is supper?" He ducked his head back in.

"Six o'clock," she answered. He patted the doorframe, waved, and headed back to his room. "Jack?" She followed him into the hallway to find him turning to her. "It's complicated. I wish there were different circumstances."

With a smile, Jack replied, "Sounds like you've thought about this a lot." He added, "Relationships are only complicated if you make them that way. Just don't figure that out when you're 81." He stepped back into his room, leaving Kat alone in the hallway.

Karl, Betty, Simon, Kat, and Gerald sat at the table in the Italian restaurant waiting for everyone else to join them. Derrick appeared around the corner with a sister hanging off each arm, escorting them to dinner. June laughed at something that was said before entering the room, and Violet shot a glare at Kat. "This needs to be you," she mouthed the words. Kat shook her head with a little blush forming on her face.

"Where's Jack? I figured he'd be down here first sampling the wine," Derrick said, pulling his chair out.

"He said he wasn't hungry and walked down to the martini bar," Gerald answered.

"Why?" Derrick asked.

Betty nudged Karl. "Go check on him."

"If he's not hungry, there's nothing I can do." Karl looked over his menu.

"Karl," Betty said his name. He knew the quicker he checked on Jack, the quicker he could eat.

"Fine. Order for me," he said as he stood up. "No cheese."

"I know, dear." Betty looked back at her menu.

Karl walked out into the cool evening air and looked both ways. Seeing a martini glass sign to his left only half a block away, he headed down the sidewalk toward the neon glow. Pulling the tarnished brass handle on the door, he walked into a dimly lit bar, finding Jack sitting at the bar alone. "You're not eating?" Karl asked.

"No, I'm good. Thanks, though," Jack answered with a bourbon glass in hand.

"OK, suit yourself." Karl turned to walk back to the restaurant. Jack watched him head to the door, then faced forward taking another sip from his glass. "Let me have a beer," Karl ordered, sitting down beside Jack.

"You're not going to eat?" Jack asked.

"No, they have cheese on everything. Beer sounds better anyway," He lied. "I know we've only known each other for a few days, but you're the kinda guy that wants to be around people. Why are you here alone?" The bartender set down a cold long neck bottle in front of Karl.

"Oh, just sometimes I like a slower pace," Jack answered.

"Well, I don't believe you. But I'm not going to pry either. Cheers," he said, holding up his bottle.

They sat quietly at the bar, the only sound a TV playing a local college game in the background. Jack faded off in thought about Delilah, wondering where she was and how her life had turned out. *From a successful business owner to a world traveler, I've managed to build a huge life and still haven't found the perfect relationship,* he thought, sipping his bourbon.

Chapter 33

The door to the martini bar swung open with Violet leading the rest of the group. The two men at the bar spun around on their bar stools as Violet yelled something about the party not starting yet.

Kat threw her arm around Jack. "Missed you two for supper."

"Figured I'd come down here and try their fried shrimp," he replied, pointing at an empty plate in front of them.

"Hey! The concert tonight is a Manhattan composer." Betty pointed to a flyer that hung near the door. "If we leave now, we could catch it." She looked at Karl.

With an eyebrow lifted, Karl answered, "I'm not in the mood for sitting in a concert hall for two hours."

Betty looked at June and Kat. "Ladies?"

"I'll be your date tonight," June ran her arm under Betty's arm and pulled her close. "Kat?" June looked at her.

"I better stay behind and get tomorrow organized," she answered.

"Don't wait up for us." June turned Betty and started walking to the door.

Violet shook her head. "Wait up," she answered in an unenthusiastic tone.

"Don't wake me when you get in," Karl yelled, but the door had already shut.

"You better go with your wife," Jack said, nodding to the door.

"Nah, she'd have made a fuss if she wanted me to go."

Gerald slid in the empty bar stool beside Jack, leaving Simon, Derrick, and Kat standing near the doorway. "I've got a phone call to make. I'll catch you guys back at the inn," Simon said and vanished out the door.

Thinking of a slick way of asking Kat to go for a walk, Derrick cleared his throat. "Would you like to take a walk?" he asked Kat.

A warm smile answered before she spoke. "Yea, that would be nice." Derrick gave a light-hearted wave to the three old men as he held the door open for Kat, and Jack gave him a thumbs up. A cool evening with a hint of salt in the air from the coast greeted them as they walked past the theater and into a newly built park with gas lanterns lighting the stone paths. The park bordered the bay that the town rested beside, and with a steady breeze, the waves could be heard crashing against a concrete wall.

"I hope they can find a way to keep Cedar Branch open," Kat said, striking up a conversation.

"I don't know. Hopefully, something will happen." Derrick wasn't sure. He took his phone out of his pocket and checked the time, but instead of putting it back, he began to flip it in the air and catch it as they continued to discuss the future of Cedar Branch. "If you hadn't been a social worker, what would you have done?" he asked, searching for conversation other than Cedar Branch.

"It's a starving profession, but I would have loved to be an artist," she answered.

He stopped and looked at her. "You paint?"

"And sketch," she smiled.

"Why haven't you shown us anything?" He was surprised.

"I didn't figure anyone would want to see them. Plus everyone is so busy at work."

"What about the art classes that are taught?"

"What about them?" she asked.

"You haven't been a part of that—why not?"

"Debbie, the teacher." She looked at him. "She's really good, and I don't want to tread on her turf."

"Not taking anything away from her, but she's not an employee of Cedar Branch. They contract her."

"I know. But I still wouldn't want to butt in on her class."

"What do you like to paint?" he asked.

"Honestly, I like to paint winter scenes. It's something about creating snow on a building or street that I like. Plus being a southern girl and all." She said with a thick southern accent, "I never got to be around snow much."

"I'd like to see your stuff... I mean paintings!" He covered his remark quickly and turned red.

Laughing Kat pulled her phone out of her pocket and coached him to a bench, showing him several pictures of her paintings. "This one is my favorite." She scrolled to a snowy scene of an old barn with a few horses scattered throughout a small pasture in front of the barn.

"Kat. These are really good."

"Thanks." She stood to continue walking, but dropped her phone. She reached down to grab the phone, and as Derrick tried to be a gentleman and grab it first, their heads butted. "Ouch." She laughed.

Also laughing, Derrick held up his hand. "You stay here." He reached for the phone on the path. Kat, not realizing what she was doing, stepped closer to Derrick, and as he handed her the phone, their faces met only inches apart. An awkward moment turned into a staring match, neither breaking a grin. She grabbed the phone, only to have Derrick close his hand, gripping her hand and the phone.

"Derrick?" she said softly, but without giving an answer, he leaned in for a kiss, and finding no resistance, they dropped the phone again.

The wind died down, leaving the echoes of crashing waves in the background and two hearts beating wildly. In the shadows of the parking lot, a grey Civic turned on its headlights and slowly drove away.

Kat felt Derrick's hand cradle the back of her neck and with the warmth of his kiss, she felt her heels leave the ground. *He's literally sweeping me off my feet*, she thought, but dared not to open her eyes. *This feels so right, but feels so wrong at the same time.*

As Derrick pulled his lips apart from hers, she slightly fell forward in a daze and opened her eyes. "Do you think this is a good idea?" she whispered.

"If you're referring to Cedar Branch code of not seeing other employees, I don't care. I might not have a job in a month. If you mean something else, well, I don't know."

"No, I'm talking about Cedar Branch," she said, thinking he had a good point.

He began second guessing himself. "Am I out of line?"

She looked at him funny. "No," she shook her head.

After picking up her phone, they locked arms and walked slowly back to the inn, not saying a word. Stopping around the corner from the entrance, Kat stepped in front of Derrick and standing on her tip toes, gave him a quick but solid kiss. "I really do need to organize tomorrow," she said.

"Yea, I better walk down to the bar and check on the men." He held her hand as she walked backwards toward the small wooden gate that led to the front door of the inn. A smile grew across her face, and she turned to walk inside with a bounce to her step and a flip of her hair. "Dang, she's good looking," Derrick said, not realizing it was out loud and that she overheard the comment.

Chapter 34

The following morning, the group gathered in the dinner hall of the old inn for breakfast. Violet sat in the middle of the table in her usual seat with a glass of tap water in front of her and Betty across the table with her tea and two crumpled up Splenda packs lying beside the glass. Everyone had already ordered when Kat made her way to the table with her file folder held close to her. She grinned at Derrick as he looked up.

"Glad our fearless leader could join us this morning!" Jack greeted her, standing to his feet.

"I don't know about fearless," she nodded toward Jack, "and I'm not sure about leader either."

Derrick slightly stood trying to be a gentlemen, but didn't want to draw attention to them either. "Coffee?" he asked, grabbing a pot of coffee that was left on the table. The room was decorated from the 20s and resembled a feminine tea room with the crocheted table cloths.

"Yes, please," she softly replied.

Betty kicked June from under the table. "What was that for?" June gave her a dirty look, but with the head nod toward Kat and Derrick from Betty, she quickly clued in and smiled back.

"Where's Karl?" Kat asked as everyone at the table sneakered at a story she hadn't heard yet.

"Well... he is still in the room. I'm sure he'll be right down." Betty answered.

Kat looked around the table, "What's so funny?"

Betty piped back in, "Oh, it's me. I got Karl's sleeping pills mixed in with the laxatives we gave those guys at the pizza place."

"Is he ok?" Kat asked not finding the humor.

"He's fine. He finally fell asleep on the toilet about 2 a.m." Betty took a sip of her sweet tea.

"So, we're back out in the water today?" Karl asked, walking up to the table with everyone giggling.

"You don't want to go fishing?" Kat asked him.

"I'd rather just eat the things. My days of working for food are over," he grumbled.

"How'd you sleep?" Violet blurted out.

Karl rolled his eye, "If my wife doesn't kill me, I'm sure you'll have your chance." The giggling broke out into a laughter.

"We always have alternate plans," Kat said. "We could drive into Houston and go shopping."

Losing interest in the story of sleeping pills and laxatives, the women at the table looked up and simultaneously replied, "Shopping!"

Kat looked back at Derrick. "Looks like shopping."

"Hang on. You didn't get the guys' vote." Karl filled up his coffee cup.

"Guys?" Kat looked at Jack and Gerald.

"I don't care either way," Gerald answered in a soft voice.

"Oh, come on, Gerald, of course you care! We men have to stick together," Karl snapped.

Gerald started to answer, but Jack interrupted him. "I vote shopping."

With a smirk on his face, Karl grumbled, "Oh, you would," and sat back in his chair.

"Would you rather be out sweating on a boat or eating ice cream in the mall?" Jack asked.

"Ice cream," Karl mumbled under his breath like a five-year-old child. Violet slapped two more pancakes and poured syrup over them until it filled her plate. Cutting a large bite of pancake, she began chewing and slurping at the same time to prevent any loss of syrup. Karl looked at her from across the table, then back at Betty. "She sounds like my coffee maker!" he said loud enough for only Betty to hear and received an elbow in the side for his effort.

"How was the concert last night?" Kat asked, drawing their attention from Violet and her pancakes.

"Oh, it was good. Wish you would have come," Betty said.

"I'm surprised you guys are awake. It wasn't late?"

"Not with Mrs. I'm Tired," June pointed at Violet.

"Well, if they're going to entertain old people, they need to wrap it up around 8:30, maybe 9. I bet they went to 10:30. That's just too late!"

"Well, it was beautiful. The composer's wife played the violin with him during one of his songs," Betty replied.

"I'm going to pull the van toward the front door," Derrick announced as he stood up.

"I'll go with you. I need to get something," Kat said, standing with him. The ladies at the table all smiled at each other, feeling love in the air.

Simon shoved the rest of the bacon in his mouth and excused himself to his room. Jack looked across the table, commenting "Could be dangerous with the three of them leaving us alone."

Karl held up his pill box. "The only danger at this table is overdosing."

"How are those socks feeling?" Jack asked Gerald.

"Like brand new."

"They are brand new! I need to get on your hand-me-down list!" Karl said.

"Gerald! We are taking you today to get new shoes." Jack looked down at Gerald's Velcro shoes.

"What's wrong with my shoes?"

"You need lace-ups." Jack held his hand up, ending the conversation. Gerald looked back down at his shoes, thinking of the ease of slipping them on and wondering why he would want lace-up shoes.

"You guys ready?" Derrick asked, walking back in. "The inn needs us to check out early. They have a professional football team's cheerleaders that will be here in an hour." He looked at his watch.

Jack leaned back in his chair. "Why on God's green earth would we want to be in a hurry?"

"I figured that would get your attention," Derrick patted Jack on the shoulder. "I'm joking. No rush, but we would like to be on the road in an hour."

"Son, you can't do that to an old man like me!" Jack grinned. The group got up and made their way to their rooms to pack.

Walking up the stairs, Karl griped to Betty, "An hour just isn't long enough."

"Sweetie, you've been on the toilet all night. I'm sure an hour is long enough."

An hour later and still under the supervision of Violet, the van was loaded and speeding toward the busy city of Houston, Texas. Derrick and Kat made several eye contacts through the rearview mirror thinking they were incognito, but each time Betty would elbow Karl and look back at June. The two-hour drive seemed as fast as Derrick's driving, which everyone but Karl had gotten used to, and before long they found themselves pulling into a parking lot at the Galleria.

"If they would have gotten a handicap sticker, we wouldn't have to park so dang far!" Karl grumbled.

"Honey, no one here is handicapped," Betty tried to reason with him.

"Keep parking in the back 40, and we'll all be handicapped before this trip is over," he muttered under his breath.

"Let's say we meet in the food court in two hours and decide where to eat," Kat said, holding the door open for everyone.

"It'll take two hours to decide where we are going to eat. Best you just tell us," Jack tipped his hat. "Gerald, my man. We are going to get you some rad shoes."

"Rad?" Gerald looked puzzled and worried.

"Wait up! I'm not just going to sit around," Karl said and followed them.

The three men walked aimlessly through the mall looking for the first shoe store they could find. Two younger women veered around them in a fast pace walk pushing two strollers. Jack cleared his throat. "Gentlemen, there are only three things that always tell the truth," he paused, letting the women gain distance, "small children, drunk people, and yoga pants!" The three men broke out into a laughter as they walked up on a sporting goods store.

A young man greeted them as they entered a store. "Good morning, gentlemen."

"Morning. Looking at lace-up tennis shoes," Jack answered.

"Lace-up?" The young man looked puzzled.

"We're in the wrong place if he doesn't know what lace-up is," Karl spouted off.

The man laughed, "I know what lace-up is. Being a sports store, that's all we offer." He led them to a wall that spanned the entire length of the store and was over eight foot tall. "Do you know what you are looking for?"

Gerald looked up at the wall and then down the store, saying quietly, "Oh, my."

"Let's consolidate this," Jack spoke up. "What's the best and most popular?"

"This year it would be these," the salesman replied, handing Jack a shoe with different color strips and laces.

Karl pulled the shoe to him, and looking at the price, asked "Is this pesos?" He looked at the man.

"No, sir."

"Good lord, we just want to buy a pair of shoes, not stock in the company." Karl pushed the shoe back to Jack.

Jack handed the shoe back, suggesting "Something a little less colorful." The salesman started searching the wall and pulled down a few white shoes with some color.

After trying on three pairs, Gerald looked at Jack. "These are nice. You should try a pair."

Karl looked at the price again. "I have a hard time believing running shoes cost so much; we need to go to Walmart."

"These are a much better shoe." The young man didn't know what to say.

"Don't mind him," Jack said. "Shoes are everything." He looked at Karl.

Chapter 35

Kat and Derrick sat with Simon in the food court waiting for the rest of the group to meet them. Simon, who was zoned out with something on his phone, was oblivious to the flirtatious conversation between the two of them. To avoid any time delay, they had made a decision to eat at a local deli only a few blocks from the Galleria. The area was buzzing with mothers and children taking a break from their midday shopping that seemed to turn into a circus in the food court. Vendors of Asian cuisine battled each other for customers as they handed out samples.

"Here come the ladies," Kat smiled and stood to greet them. "Did you guys find everything you needed?"

"And then some," June said, holding up her bags.

Betty sat in the chair next to Derrick, panting out of breath. "Good lord, this place is big." She started searching around her pockets and in her bag. "Where did I put my phone?" Violet tapped on the table in front of her, showing

Betty her phone where she had set it down. "That's not my phone," she replied, picking it up, then laughing, "Oh, ha, sorry." She placed it in her bag.

"Where are the men?" June asked.

Derrick pointed to the three men chasing the restaurant vendors around the food court, eating as many free samples as they could muster. Betty waved, getting Karl's attention, and motioned them over to the table. Walking around a group of teens, the three men headed toward the table as if they had just conquered the Roman Empire, all three wearing the same brand new shoes.

"Those Asians act like they own the damn restaurant!" Karl fussed with a mouth full of samples.

Violet lifted an eyebrow. "Looks like you guys are going to a Sadie Hawkins dance," she commented, pointing to their shoes.

"You bought shoes?" Betty asked Karl as if he never bought shoes.

He threw a thumb over his shoulder, pointing at Jack. "He made me."

"Made him?" Jack looked at Betty. "It was the cute little sales lady that talked him into it. I never knew Karl could flirt like that."

"Flirt!" Karl fought to get the word out, trying to defend himself. "There wasn't a sales lady! He's making that up," Karl shouted above the noise in the food court. Jack winked at Betty.

"Now, now. He's just picking at you," Betty laughed, pulling Karl down to an empty chair.

"Where are we eating?" June asked Kat.

"There is a nice deli just a few blocks from here," she answered.

"Well, we're not eating in this daycare!" Violet looked over the area littered with children. "What on earth are all these women thinking, having all these kids?"

"They're thinking about men—that's what," June answered.

"You'd think coming here would encourage safe sex or in this case no sex!"

Derrick stood and handed the keys to Simon. "How about we take all this sex talk to the deli," he suggested.

"Oh? You want to talk about sex?" Violet elbowed Kat while looking at Derrick. Both Derrick and Kat turned as red as Karl's new shoes.

Stuttering, Derrick pushed Simon toward the door, saying, "Simon and I are going to get the van."

"I can get it," Simon replied.

"I'll help," Derrick said, trying to escape his embarrassment.

While waiting on the van to pick them up at the door, Jack instructed Gerald and Karl to fan out and canvas the area for more samples. Kat and the ladies watched as the food vendors did their best to run from the three men that kept sampling from their trays. Kat's phone buzzed with a text from Derrick saying they were at the door.

Kat had gathered everyone and started toward the door when she noticed Betty still sitting at the table. "Are you ready?" she asked, walking back to the table, but received only a blank stare from Betty. "Betty, you ready?"

"Ready for what?" Betty asked.

"To go eat."

Betty looked down at her purse, then back to Kat. "We just ate. Are the kids with you?"

"Kids?"

"Yes. We can't go without the children," she replied with a strange expression.

Kat leaned down and look at her, "Betty, are you ok?" She didn't receive an answer and glanced in Karl's direction. He was watching from across the food court as if reading Kat's mind and made his way toward them quickly. "She's confused," Kat told him as he walked up.

"Betty, what's the matter?" Karl took her hand.

"This nice lady is waiting with me to take the kids back to the house."

"Sweetheart, we don't own the house anymore," he answered. Betty looked up with a confused expression. He pulled on her hand, saying, "Help me get her up." Together they got Betty to her feet and started toward the van. The others were heading out unaware.

Betty stopped shy of entering the van. "I'm not ready," she said.

Kat shot Derrick a stern gaze to gain his attention, telling him, "She's confused." Derrick climbed out and walked around the van to help. "Maybe we should call 911?" Kat asked, catching the attention of everyone already loaded in the van.

Without hesitation, Derrick pulled his cell phone and dialed while walking to the front of the van to talk to the 911 operator. Within moments, the sound of a single siren rang throughout the streets and parking lot of the Galleria.

As the paramedics helped Betty onto the stretcher, Derrick instructed Kat, "Go with the ambulance and I'll take everyone to the hotel. I'm sure they'll let us check in, and once I get everyone checked in, I'll head to the hospital." She nodded, acknowledging his orders, and helped the paramedics get Betty into the back of the ambulance. Karl looked on like a helpless child, so Derrick helped him in the front seat and assured him everything was going to be OK.

Once at the hospital, they took Betty into the emergency room and Karl and Kat to the admissions office. Kat pulled Betty's file from her shoulder bag with insurance cards and a full list of her medication. "This should be everything."

"Can I go back to see her?" Karl asked. The nurse checking them in smiled and asked another nurse to take him back. He walked into the room to find Betty hooked up to a monitor, nasal cannula in her nose, and a young nurse starting an IV. Karl took a deep breath and made his way to Betty's side, gently holding her hand. She opened her eyes and smiled at him, giving him a small sigh of relief. This was a sight that wasn't uncommon with either one of them, but something that was coming too often.

"Mr. Rutherfurd?" a middle-aged gentleman in a white coat asked.

"Yes."

"We are going to take good care of Mrs. Rutherfurd, so don't worry," the doctor replied. "Do you guys prepare your pills in advance?" he asked.

"Prepare?"

"Do you have a pill box?"

"Yes. It should be in her purse." Karl dug through Betty's brown leather coach handbag and handed both pill dispensers to the doctor, who studied the medicine sheet Kat had presented. He looked in Betty's pill dispenser counting pill with the tip of his pen and then back to the sheet.

Shaking his head, "Looks like she is taking a mild form of Bactrim for a urinary tract infection," he glanced at Karl.

"I believe that's right."

The doctor smiled, giving Karl relief. "I believe she has mixed up her blood pressure medicine with the Bactrim. No Bactrim and twice the blood pressure. I take it she organizes the meds?"

"She does," Karl answered thinking back to the sleeping pill and laxative mix-up.

"I would suggest you two get help organizing the meds. UTI is a common cause of memory loss in our older age. I'll prescribe her something a little stronger so we can kick this infection, and I'm sure she'll be fine," the doctor said, writing on her file.

"When will she get better with her memory?"

"Let's let her rest, and I bet after a good nap and some fluids, she'll be back to her normal self." He shook Karl's hand and disappeared to his next patient. Karl walked to the waiting room to give the news to Kat and found both Derrick and Jack sitting with her.

"They're going to keep her a few hours to rest and watch her, but she'll be fine," Karl said.

"That's good news," Jack answered ahead of everyone.

"What are you doing here?" Karl asked. "Figured you'd be conversing at a bar somewhere."

"Nah, too early for that. Plus I hear there's some good-looking nurses around here." He scanned the area. Karl rolled his eyes.

Chapter 36

Derrick and Jack sat in the waiting room of the ER carrying on a casual conversation about New York and the real-estate world. Derrick was not only surprised at the size of the empire Jack had grown, but the fact that he gave it all to his son. "I've tried to live simple and not focus on the materialistic things in life," he said.

Karl returned to the waiting area, saying, "You guys don't need to hang around here. She's resting, and we probably won't leave for another hour or two."

"I don't mind," Derrick answered.

Jack looked at Derrick. "You've got things to do and other people to watch. Violet alone is enough for one person. I'll stay with the Rutherfurds."

"Nah, I —" he was interrupted.

"Plus you got a sweet thing to court," Jack added. Derrick looked at Karl, who was nodding his head in agreement, and received a wave toward the door.

"Call me as soon as she is being discharged. I'm only 15 minutes away."

Jack pulled a chess board on a small table he'd been eyeing toward two empty chairs. "How good are you?" he asked Karl.

"I know how to play," Karl answered, quickly taking a seat and not mentioning having been in a chess club for nearly 15 years. Jack read right off that Karl was playing him and grinned at his shark attitude. The two men played several games, and during the third game Karl softly gave Jack a *thank you* without looking at him.

"Don't mention it." Jack thought back to the night before in the bar.

After a couple of hours of beating Jack and a call to Derrick, Karl wheeled Betty to the van waiting under the ER awning. Both Derrick and Kat, who were previously holding hands, were waiting. "My, I'm receiving a wonderful welcome," Betty smiled.

"How do you feel?" Kat helped her out of the wheelchair and into the van.

"Like a million dollars. I hope I didn't ruin everyone's afternoon."

"Not at all. Everyone is soaking up some sun poolside. I think it was a much-needed relaxing afternoon," Kat answered.

At the hotel, the valet took the van from Derrick, and the five of them cut through the pool to visit with everyone. Entering the pool area under a trellis of Wisteria, they met the group sitting poolside as a young waiter took orders for appetizers and drinks. Everyone but Violet was out of the pool, and once they were noticed, June announced their arrival. "There they are!"

Everyone turned to see them stroll in, and Violet climbed out of the pool. Jack, Karl, and Derrick stopped cold in their tracks. "What in the hell is she wearing?" Karl said, his jaw falling open.

"I'm not sure she is wearing *anything*," Jack said, clueless.

Derrick remained silent. Of all the years taking trips, he'd never seen someone quite as comfortable wearing a string bikini as Violet. Karl stopped Betty "She needs to put some clothes on," he said, loud enough for the five of them to hear.

"Oh hush," Betty replied. "If she's comfortable enough to wear it, then you should be comfortable enough to be around it." Betty and Kat continued walking toward the group.

"*Round* is the key word here, gentlemen," Jack said with his hand covering his mouth.

"What's the prognosis?" Violet asked, drying herself off.

"A lot of flab," Karl blurted out. "I mean a lot of rest." He quickly recovered his words, shaking his head.

"Violet, with your attire, I assume you're comfortable with nude beaches," Jack said, adjusting his hat.

She smiled in his direction. "You asking?"

"If you know of one," he shot back.

"The manager here said no European sun bathing," Violet joked.

"I'm sure that disappointed Gerald." Jack glanced at him and received a halfhearted smile.

"Oh, you should come home with us; she parades around the house in the nude like she's Eve from the Bible," June replied.

"Something to look forward to at Cedar Branch," Karl said, rolling his eyes.

Betty elbowed him in the side. "We are going up to change," she announced.

The waiter returned with a tray of food and drinks on his shoulder. "Sir, would you like anything," he looked at Jack, setting the tray down.

"How about a New Orleans Hurricane," Jack said as he started to unbutton his shirt.

"Yes, sir."

Jack threw his shirt across the back of a lounge chair and began unbuttoning his pants. "Jack?" Karl shouted.

Jack gave him a funny look, pulling his pants down to reveal his shorts. "Relax," he said.

"You always wear shorts under your pants?" Derrick asked.

"Son, at my age you can lose anything, including your trousers. Like a Boy Scout, always be prepared." He sat in the chair beside Gerald.

"Good lord, I need to rest," Karl said, heading toward the elevators.

"You two go change and come back to join us," June said to Derrick and Kat, who didn't give it a second thought and followed the Rutherfurds to the elevator.

A young couple entered the pool through the same double doors and looked over the pool, seeing Violet, then looked at each other and walked back into the hotel. "Light weights," Violet said.

"So, Gerald, you were in the hotel business. Ever had trouble at the pool with people staying dressed?" Jack asked. Gerald remained silent, and a closer glance from Jack revealed that Gerald had dozed off.

Moments later, Derrick returned and set his towel in the empty chair beside Jack. "I need to ask the front desk a question. Be right back." He ducked in the lobby, just missing Kat, who exited from the elevators and walked out to the pool. She laid her bag beside June and slipped out of her flip flops.

Sticking her toes in the water, Kat shivered and said, "How in the world can you swim in that water? It's freezing."

"Honey," Violet answered, "at this age and with this much body, your temperature gauge stops working." She laughed.

Derrick started back out the double doors, but was halted in his tracks. Kat unbuttoned her shorts, letting them drop to the concrete floor, and pulled her t-shirt over her head, revealing her toned body covered by a one-piece teal bathing suit. She pulled her hair back in a ponytail, adjusted her sunglasses, and climbed into the chair beside June. Derrick felt his heart stop. After catching his breath, he walked to his chair, unaware of the eyes behind the sunglasses following him. He pulled his shirt off and threw it near his shoes. "Jack, this is the life," Derrick said.

"You said it," Jack answered under the fedora hat pulled over his face. Kat caught her breath as she cut her eyes toward Derrick. They locked eyes and gave each other a smile.

Chapter 37

Hearing a light knock at her hotel door, Kat left the towel she was drying her hair with draped across her shoulders and quickly slipped into shorts and a t-shirt. Karl was standing in the doorway as she opened the door. "Hey, Karl. Everything OK?"

"Yea, but with the doctor asking Betty not to organize our pills any more, could you check to see if these are correct? I'm not interested in sleeping on the toilet anymore." He handed her a large zip lock bag of pill bottles and two weekly pill dispensers. "Pharmacies don't have anything on us," he smiled.

"Don't worry about it," Kat replied giggling, closing the door as he turned to walk back to his room. She placed the bag and dispensers on her bed and went back to drying her hair. Leaned over and brushing her hair while running the dryer, she heard another knock, not as light as before. She opened the door again expecting Karl but this time found Derrick. "Hey." She grinned.

"Oh, I'm sorry. I didn't mean to catch you at a bad time." He started to back up.

"Don't be silly, come in." She stepped to the side and back into the bathroom to finish drying her hair with a slightly faster heart rate.

"Whose pills are those?" he yelled above the dryer.

She stuck her head out of the bathroom, saying, "The Rutherfurds."

He made his way to the bathroom doorway, and while she looked at him upside down, "What's up?" Kat yelled over the hairdryer.

"Checking on tomorrow plans," he said.

She turned off the dryer and stood upright, "You're wanting to know about the schedule?" she smiled, hoping there was more to his visit.

Turning a light shade of red, Derrick replied, "Well, I just wanted to . . ."

"It's OK," She interrupted him dropping the hair drier to the floor. To both of their surprise they simultaneously locked arms around each other followed by their lips colliding together. In the heat of the moment, Derrick back pedaled to the bed, where he fell back with Kat landing on top of him. He could feel the wet tips of her hair tangling around his neck as their kiss settled in more passionate. She felt butterflies in her stomach as if it was her first kiss.

In between breaths Derrick looked over at the clock on the table and realized they were late for supper. He pulled on the back of her neck to lure her down for another kiss, but felt resistance, "We can't be late for supper," she whispered.

"Why not?" he answered, knowing she was right. Kat rolled off of him and sat up trying to catch her breath and struggling to wipe the grin off her face. "All right, I'll go reserve a table." He stood only to find Kat wrapped back around him with her head buried in his chest, so he drew her in close with his arms. She could not only hear but feel his heartbeat, a beat that felt right and safe.

With a quick peck on the lips, Kat whispered, "I'll finish getting ready." She released him and walked back into the bathroom tingling all over.

Derrick stepped out of her room, pulling the door shut, and ran into Jack, who gave a big smile. "Yep, I'd say to hell with the dating rule too."

"We were just—"

Jack raised his hand. "No need to explain. You going downstairs?"

Derrick nodded his head *yes*, and together they walked down the steps to the restaurant. The hotel was set in an elegant manner with large colorful floral arrangements scattered throughout the lobby and meeting rooms. A deep, thick red carpet led to the front desk, with several people standing in line to check in, and the bellmen scrambled to collect everyone's luggage. Jack put his hand on Derrick's shoulder and followed him into the restaurant. A marble bar curved with the layout of the area and bordered the wall leading out to the pool.

"Well, we were wondering where you guys were!" Violet yelled above the conversations at other tables.

"We were catching up on old times," Jack winked at Derrick.

"Where is Kat? I figured you were with her," Betty said, craning to see the doorway.

"She'll be right here." Derrick looked at Violet's glass of ice water. "I see you got your ice water."

She rolled her eyes. "Don't get me started."

"Good lord, everyone is almost here, let's order," Karl snapped.

A waiter overheard Karl and stepped up to the table. "Are you ready?" he said with a smile. Everyone stared at their menus, but not a word was heard. "I'll give you some more time," the waiter said, stepping back out of the way.

"Gerald, how are those new tennis shoes feeling?" Kat smiled, walking up to the table.

"Took me half an hour to tie them. I think I'm missing my old shoes already," he replied.

"They'll stretch out before long and you'll be able to slip right into them." She patted him on the shoulder.

Violet pointed her fork at Gerald. "That's a good way to roll an ankle. My friend back in Arkansas did the same thing, and she couldn't walk for two weeks."

Karl rolled his eyes again. "Good grief, just loosen the laces."

Jack waved at the young waiter. "Do you have a bottle of Garrison Brothers? Cowboy Bourbon?"

The waiter smiled, "Yes, sir, we do."

"We'll take a bottle," Jack said, looking back down at his menu.

The group snacked on calamari and firecracker shrimp while Derrick, Karl, Simon, and Kat sipped on the bottle of bourbon that Jack had ordered. Kat figured she had better try it now and doubted she'd ever have another chance to sample a two-hundred-dollar bottle of whiskey. After eating and laughing at the stories that traded during their meal, the group settled back in their chairs.

Jack leaned over to Gerald's glass. "You need another?"

With his hand over the glass, Gerald declined. "No, no. I've had my quota."

A glass slid to a stop in front of Jack. "Not me," Violet smiled.

Pouring a shot, Jack replied, "Better go easy on this, it's like an Indian. It'll sneak up on you."

"You need to come to Arkansas and try some of the local stash," she replied.

With a hand in the air, Jack said, "No, I've heard."

Gerald climbed out of his chair, and saying, "I've got to get some fresh air," he started toward the door.

"Do you want some company?" Kat asked. She received a smile for her answer and together she and Gerald walked out into the evening Texas air. Cutting through the pool area and out into the street, they walked a few blocks looking in the windows of the local shops and taverns. "Busy down here," she commented.

"Yep," Gerald responded.

"Are you excited about moving into Cedar Branch?" she asked.

"I believe so. I've been lonely here the last four or five months."

"You should move in with Jack," Kat laughed and nudged him with her shoulder.

She got a laugh from him. "I'm not *that* lonely."

Kat started worrying about what was in store for Cedar Branch and her job. She hated to ask questions like "are you happy to move in" when it could only be temporary. It was killing her that she had to keep quiet, something she wasn't really good at doing.

"It's a beautiful hotel we are staying in," she said, trying to change her thoughts.

"Yes, it's one of the nicest in Houston," Gerald replied.

"You were in the hotel business, right?"

"I was. This was actually one of the hotels we tried to buy, but the owners wouldn't budge."

"Do you miss the business?"

"I do. With my family, you don't really ever retire. I enjoyed buying and rebuilding hotels that were in tough times."

Kat smiled in deep thought.

Chapter 38

Karl and Jack sat at the bar, entertained by two young businessmen doing their best to pick up two beautiful young women dressed to kill. Jack nudged Karl, "Those boys don't have a clue that a thousand dollars would cut out the small talk and land them in their rooms."

"Goodness, what happened to dinner and a show?" Karl looked past Jack at the foursome.

Jack turned with a puzzled look. "They're professionals."

"Who's professional at what?"

"Karl, you're killing me. The girls. They are high-end call girls." Jack took a sip of his bourbon.

"Hookers?" Karl gasped.

Jack waved him back down in his seat, "You don't have to announce it to the whole restaurant."

"How do you know?"

Jack grinned. "I've been around long enough."

"We need to warn those young men," Karl started off his bar stool.

Jack quickly grabbed his arm, "Let them figure it out. Who knows? They might be able to afford them."

Karl couldn't stop watching the foursome and observed the ladies laugh at the ignorance of the young men until one of them told the guys their price. The young man had the same look on his face as Karl did. Simon stopped at the bar. "Are Kat and Gerald back?"

"Haven't seen them. Want a glass?" Jack asked.

"No, thank you. Do you mind giving her the keys to the van? I'd give them to Derrick, but he's working out in the fitness area."

"Sure," Jack said, confused. "Where are you going?"

"I'm turning in early," Simon replied and walked back to the elevators.

Lifting an eyebrow, Jack looked at Karl and jiggled the keys. "Night on the town?"

Still watching the girls, Karl said "Sure," agreeing without knowing what he agreed to.

Jack waved over the bar tender. "What's the swankiest dance club in town?"

The bar tender looked at him for a second. "Well, the hottest club right now is the Oyster Club, but unless you know someone there is a long line to get in. There is another club on—"

Jack stopped him. "Where is the Oyster Club?'

"Corner of Milam and Seville."

"You got a number?" Jack asked him, not giving him time to say anything else. The bar tender nodded, walked back to the computer, pulled up the phone number and wrote it down for Jack. Jack slid his bottle of bourbon toward the bar tender. "Can you shelf this for me?" he asked, and dropped a twenty-dollar tip on the bar.

"Where are you going?" Karl chimed in.

"Round up the troops. We're going out." Jack stopped and looked back at Karl, adding, "Don't say anything to Derrick or Kat and let's meet at the van in 15 minutes."

"They need to know we are leaving."

"Not tonight—tell them everyone is turning in early."

"Where are you going?" Karl asked.

"To get Gerald and make a call." And Jack disappeared around the corner.

Karl headed to his room to get Betty and collect the Stevens sisters from their room. Betty was hesitant to go and was surprised at Karl's willingness to follow Jack, but after a few seconds of thinking about it, she grabbed her sweater. Violet and June followed them out to the van, where Jack and Gerald waited for them.

"Guys! We're going to the hippest night club in town. I don't think they'll let us in wearing workout clothes and the attire from *Leave It to Beaver*." Jack shook his head.

"What do you suggest?" June asked.

Jack rubbed his hands together. "You four are executives from Paramount Pictures that are visiting a film produced by Gerald Schooler. You need to dress like that."

"What the hell are you talking about?" Karl asked.

"I already called the club; they are expecting six highly acclaimed managerial executives that are in town visiting a 90-million-dollar film being shot in Houston."

Betty smiled and grabbed June's hand. "Come on, let's get changed. This should be fun."

"Good grief! We're going to jail!" Karl reluctantly followed the ladies back upstairs to change. They passed Derrick standing in the lobby with a perplexed look on his face. "I have the same damn look all the time," Karl commented as he walked past him. Derrick watched them disappear into the elevator and thought it best not to ask about that peculiar act.

Twenty minutes, later the group snuck back down through the lobby and out to the back parking lot, where Gerald and Jack were sitting in the van. Everyone started to climb in, but "Wait!" Violet ordered.

"It will be OK. Worst thing is that we not get in the club," Jack said, sitting in the driver's seat.

"It's not that. If you're driving and Gerald is riding shotgun, then Karl and June need to be in the next seat with Betty and me in the third row."

"Good lord—"

Betty pushed Karl into the van, interrupting his fit. "Do you know where you're going?" June asked Jack.

Putting the van into drive, Jack just said, "Yep."

"I hope Simon doesn't come down to look for his bag." Karl held up Simon's backpack. Everyone looked back, simultaneously blew it off, and faced back front. Karl shrugged his shoulders, and as he set the bag back on the floor, something fell out of the side pocket. Karl picked up a small wooden pipe. "What is this?" he asked Violet.

"Where did you get that?" she asked. Karl pointed to the bag. Violet snatched the bag and unzipped the top, digging through Simon's backpack.

"What are you doing?" Karl asked.

Violet pulled out and presented a zip lock bag of green herb-like substance. "Ha! We found Simon's stash," she proudly showed the van.

"Good lord!" Karl shouted. "I knew that boy was up to no good. Stop the van!"

Jack slammed on the brakes and turned around to see Karl throwing a fit in the back seat. "Karl, it's OK. It's just reefer," Jack said.

Karl climbed over the seat. "I'm not going anywhere with pot in the van. I can see it now, all of us in the police station with Simon's grass."

"Yea, and your prints all over the pipe. How are you going to explain that?" Violet taunted him.

"Betty! We are getting out," Karl's voice went up two octaves. Everyone climbed out of the van, leaving it stopped in the middle of the parking lot.

"Here, give me the bag." Jack walked over to a nearby dumpster and hid the backpack behind it. Walking back up to the group, he added, "I'll give it to Simon when we get back. Now can we at least act like executives?"

Violet rolled her eyes toward Karl. "If you can get our drama queen back in the van."

Jack stepped in before Karl had time to respond. "Come on, nothing is going to happen." One by one, everyone got back into the van, and Jack once again placed it in drive and started out of the parking lot.

"Do you even have a driver's license?" Karl asked from the back.

"Y'all hang on! I want to try something I saw in a cartoon!" Jack yelled. Karl took a deep breath, then felt for his pulse.

Chapter 39

As the van circled the block for the second time, Karl told Jack, "Drop us off and we'll wait for you to park."

"Do you think they'll let you in after the Cedar Branch Retirement van drops you off?" Jack asked, searching for a parking place.

"You have a point," Karl replied. "There!" Karl pointed to a vacant spot on the road. Jack pulled up to the parking place and started to parallel park. After pulling up and blocking traffic for the third time, he started to pull away.

"Don't leave! I'll park it," Violet demanded and opened the side door. Jack put the van in park and climbed out, still blocking two cars and a truck. The two cars sped by, but the truck stopped beside them, the driver rolling down his window and yelling, "Hey, old man, either learn to drive or turn your license in."

"Jerk!" Violet yelled back.

"Really. I don't have trouble driving. Just parking," Jack

smiled, not bothered by the rude comment. Violet whipped the van into the parking space and climbed back out while the others filed out and gathered on the sidewalk. "OK, remember to act like executives," Jack said.

"And how do movie executives act?" Karl asked.

"Best thing is not to say anything. You don't have time to talk," Jack said. The six of them walked the two blocks to the entrance of the club. A line of young, trendy people stretched around the corner, staring at the six retirees as they strolled past. One of the young men in line took a picture of them, and Jack held his hand in front of his face blocking the photo. With that action, ten other people took out their phones and started taking pictures.

Betty tucked her arm under Karl's arm and pulled him close, smiling. "I feel important."

"I feel like an idiot. We'll never get in the club, and why in the world do we want to? I can barely hear in a normal setting, much less with music blaring," Karl said out of the corner of his mouth.

Jack walked up to a large, puzzled-looking man holding a clip board. "Schooler party," Jack explained.

The man just stared at him. "I think you have the wrong place," he answered in a deep tone.

Jack looked up at the sign. "This is the Oyster Club."

"Yes, a night club," the doorkeeper answered. Jack didn't say anything and just stared at him. The man took a deep breath, and with a sigh he examined the clip board. "Oh, dang. Mr. Schooler?" he asked Jack.

"No, I'm his acting manager and lifelong friend. This is Mr. Schooler." Jack pointed to Gerald, who stood behind him with a nonchalant, take-it-or-leave-it demeanor.

The man moved the red velvet rope, giving the group access to the front door, and holding the mic that was pinned to his shirt, called for someone to meet them at the door. "Again, sorry, Mr. Schooler. Really glad you are visiting us tonight."

Betty tried her best to keep quiet, but she couldn't hold it in any longer, "Have you ever acted for film?" she asked.

"What are you doing?" Karl elbowed her.

"Yes ma'am, a little. My brother and I were in a commercial one time," he smiled, letting his tough-guy attitude down.

"I bet we have a spot for you in this movie we are filming—" she tried to add, but Karl pushed her in the door and smiled at the man.

Placing the rope back, he closed the door with a big smile and hopeful dreams of starring in Betty's movie, and turning back to the crowd, his tough guy demeanor came back and he crossed his arms.

"Hey! Why do the old people get to go in? I'm not interested if it's geriatric night," said a small guy standing in line.

"Give a little respect to the largest film company and their executives," the gatekeeper replied. "Now get back to the end of the line for being a punk!" He waved him on.

Inside the club, music was pounding to a swift beat and lights swirled throughout the building with laser precision and colorful arrays. Jack led the lost group into the main area and stopped just shy of a large section of steps leading to the dance floor. The manager, a well-dressed man with a little blue blazer, approached them. "Jack?" he asked.

"You have good intuition," Jack replied.

"I wish I did, but you said you'd be wearing a fedora

hat," the man smiled.

"Ha, I did." Jack removed his hat. Appearing from the side, a young lady in a short, tight dress offered to take his hat and anything else the group would like to check in.

"Mr. Schooler, it's an honor to have you here. I reserved you our finest table; please follow me."

"Table?" Gerald asked Jack. Jack shrugged his shoulders, and the group followed the man—except Violet, who veered off to the DJ's booth.

The manager showed the group a bar table surrounded with high-back bar stools and elevated on a platform to see most of the club. The manager leaned over to an assistant, and without the group hearing, he ordered, "Make sure this crowd inside and out knows that Paramount Pictures is here, good for business." He winked, then turned back to Gerald. "What movie are you filming here in Houston?"

Puzzled at what to reply, "A Gene Autry film," Gerald responded. Jack looked at him with eyes wide open and a startled look.

The young man, clueless about who Gene Autry was, replied, "That's great. I can't wait to see it. 3D?"

"Yep," Gerald replied, not hearing what he asked.

Another young man walked up and pulled the manger's shoulder. "There's some lady asking our DJ Mike to play a Frank Sinatra song. Are we taking requests now? Mike can't get rid of her, so do you want me to throw her out?"

"Play the song!" the manager ordered. The young man looked confused and walked back. Moments later, the club echoed with Sinatra and Crosby. The crowd looked at each other, then within seconds broke out into song with them.

The DJ just shook his head with amazement.

Violet walked up to the table. "One song! That's all I asked."

"When they figure out who we are and that Gene Autry died almost twenty years ago, we are certainly going to jail," Karl yelled over the music to the entire table.

Jack held up a glass. "Until then, here's to tonight!" The group raised their drinks along with Betty's unsweet tea and Violet's tap water.

A beautiful young lady in a skimpy dress approached Jack. "So, how do I get in a Paramount movie?" she smiled.

"A dance would be a good start." Jack stood up and held his arm out to escort her to the dance floor.

"All joking aside, I really am an actress and would love any advice you could give," she boldly replied, stepping on the dance floor.

Jack leaned in for her to hear him. "Sweetheart, all joking aside, we're escapees from a retirement center."

She froze in place and gazed at him with a blank stare, then broke out into a laugh. "Oh my gosh, for a second you had me," she laughed and began moving to the music.

Laughing, Jack shook his head. *Only in my younger days*, he thought.

Chapter 40

During the evening, the group received royal treatment from the staff and many of the bystanders that had heard the news that all six were big wigs in the movie industry. Gerald sat in his chair beside June, smiling at the young people and their attire, but unable to hear anything but distortion from the massive speakers that hung above on rafters. June, who was in the same predicament with Gerald in not hearing anything, developed her own style of sign language that the others picked up on quickly. A hand turning up toward the mouth symbolizing a drink and a thumb over the shoulder with both eyebrows dancing up and down meant a hunk.

"It's almost 11 o'clock. How long are we staying?" Karl shouted at Betty.

Jake overheard the question and replied, "Do you have somewhere to be tomorrow?"

"I don't want to be late for the funeral," Karl yelled back.

A questioning expression grew on Jack's face. "What funeral?"

"Mine, if we don't get out of here!"

When Jack waved over the young man waiting on them and asked to close his tab, Karl threw a ten dollar bill on the table. "What's this for?" Jack asked.

"Water and tea."

With a patient smile, Jack shoved it in his pocket and signed the bill on the plastic tray holding his credit card. The group followed the manager out, receiving their jackets and Jack's fedora hat from the same young lady who had taken them. The manager turned to Karl, asking, "Can I signal for your limo?"

Karl turned to Betty. "What the hell is he saying? We're in limbo?"

Betty gently grabbed the manager's wrist. "We parked down the block. We like to travel incognito." She winked at him and received a smile.

With the door opening to the exit of six elderly people from the dance club, the crowd standing in line lit up; they had received word about Paramount Pictures in the house. The sexy young girl that Jack had been dancing with pushed by the manager and the doorman to hand Jack a note. "Here's my number. Please call when you start filming the Egyptian Nile you told me about." She slipped a card in his jacket pocket and kissed him on the cheek.

Jack winked at Karl. "I'm 81, but I still got it," he bragged.

"That's nothing to boast about—you could still get VD too," Karl mumbled under his breath, perturbed about staying out so late. Walking past the long line, they stumbled upon two young men wearing a wardrobe of tweed jackets and fedora hats. Karl gasped for a breath. "We'll never hear the end of this," he said to Betty.

"You see that!" Jack yelled to the group. "Keep your clothes long enough, and they come back in style," he proudly boasted and elbowed Gerald. "It's been a good night. Got a number and learned I'm still in fashion, all in one night." Gerald smiled happily in his Members Only jacket and khaki pants.

"Do you actually think you're going to get lucky with that phone number?" Karl spat off.

"Karl, my good man. I've come to the realization that getting lucky at my age is finding my car in the mall parking lot." Everyone started to laugh, "Then again getting lucky is finding the truck that belonged to the guy who yelled at us before we went in the club." Jack pointed at the blue four-door parking across the street.

Violet looked at Jack. "You know we're not going to let that jerk get away with calling you an old man." She had a devious look in her eye.

"He *is* an old man. Now let's go before we all go to jail," Karl barked.

Jacked glanced back at Gerald, who only shrugged his shoulders that he was with the group, then back to Violet, June, and Betty, who were smiling like a bunch of middle school kids getting into something mischievous. Jack walked over to the truck with Violet, June, and Betty hot on his tail to see what he would do. "We could let the air out of the tires," June giggled.

"Nah, we need to do something about his parking," Jack said, looking around the truck.

"Parking?" Betty asked.

"Since he made a reference about *my* parking," Jack smiled.

"We could back our van up and hook up the truck and pull it out of the parking space," Violet said, holding up a long chain she found in the back of the truck. Everyone smiled vindictively.

"Oh, good lord!" Karl gasped for his breath across the street. "Here comes the fuzz!" He yelled to the group.

"Well, don't announce it everyone!" Jack yelled back.

Two patrol officers pulled up with bewildered expressions at seeing two old men on one side of the street and four other elderly people on the opposite side. "Everything OK?" the officer on the passenger side asked Jack with his window rolled down.

"Yep! Just helping these fine ladies cross the street," Jack replied.

The officer looked at the other officer with a questioning look, then back to Jack. "Do you mind me asking what you folks are doing out at this hour?"

"Just left the Oyster Bar," Jack said, pointing up the block.

"OK? You folks be careful tonight," the officer replied, and the patrol car slowly pulled away. "Something fishy about that," he said to the driver.

Jack and the ladies hurried across the street and quickly walked to their van, everyone piling in like they were being chased. "Well it was a good idea," Betty said.

"What was a good idea?" Karl questioned. But before he could get an answer, Jack backed the van into the small parking lot and close to the blue truck.

With a smile, Violet said, "I'll get the chain."

"I don't know what you're doing, but this is a bad idea!" Karl shook his head.

"You stay in the driver seat! June and I will hook up the truck," Violet ordered and bailed out the side door before anyone could answer. Betty followed, with Karl still in his seat covering his eyes and praying out loud.

"Hey, Karl, while you're talking to the big guy upstairs, ask him if he can send that young sexy thing to my room tonight," Jack laughed.

A brief second later, Karl opened his hands, eyeing Jack. "God asked Jack who!"

Around the back, Violet crawled under the van and wrapped the chain around the frame, while June only wrapped the back bumper of the truck with chain. "That should get it—let's go!" The three ladies barreled back into the van.

"All good?" Jack asked.

"Yep, I left some slack in the chain, so you can give it a good jolt to move that big truck," Violet instructed.

Jack backed up a couple of feet to get some more running room before the chain would tighten, and just as they prepared to take off the patrol car returned. "Everyone get down!" Jack ordered. Everyone ducked below view of the officers.

The patrol car stopped briefly and examined the parking job of the white van with Cedar Branch Retirement written on the side. "We could go find the old people and figure out what this is all about or go look for drunk drivers," the officer driving observed.

"It would be less paper work for a drunk driver," the other officer replied. The patrol car pulled away.

"That was close! Let's get out of here," Violet yelled. Jack hunched over the steering wheel and slammed the gearshift into drive, punching the gas pedal to the floor. Within three feet the chain tightened, lifting the back of the van off the ground with all the force. A loud crash echoed throughout the streets, causing the people in line to get in the night club to turn their attention to the white van sitting a half block away.

Everyone in the van stared at each other with a look of shock. "Don't just sit here—go!" Violet ordered, pushing Jack's shoulder. Jack floored the van, and with the chain hooked around the frame and the V8 engine under the hood, they pulled the bumper off the truck. Jack swerved and fishtailed the van entering the street and still hunched over the steering wheel flew by the night club with everyone staring. Sparks from the bumper being dragged lit the night, and a scraping sound echoed through the block.

The manager and doorman were still standing where the group had left them, and as the white van with Cedar Branch Retirement Community written on the side passed by with the bumper dragging behind, Betty waved at them from her window. They looked at each other, then back to the taillights of the van as it swung around the corner. "Was that... ?" the manager asked.

"I'm not sure," the doorman replied, feeling they had been duped.

Chapter 41

D errick picked up a long-sleeved shirt he had been wearing all day off the bed and pressed it against his face, smelling to see if there was any life left in it. "It'll be all right," he said, convincing himself that it didn't smell too bad. He had waited for everyone to get settled in their rooms, hoping that most would be asleep, before he visited Kat. Even though everyone was vocal about them dating, he didn't want to press the issue or give them something to talk about. He opened the door and glanced out to see if anyone was in the hall. Realizing he was alone, he walked lightly toward her room.

He knocked effortlessly with the back of his hand to avoid being too loud, and he could hear Kat walking toward the door. With the door swinging open, Derrick wasn't prepared for what greeted him: Standing in the doorway was a medium-height, short haircut, rim-glasses guy. Derrick's first thought was he had the wrong room, but after glancing at the room number, he looked back at the guy with a dumbfounded expression. "I'm sorry; I was looking for Kat."

Stretching his hand out, the man said, "You must be Derrick? It's nice to meet you."

Derrick reluctantly shook his hand. "Hello?"

"I hope my visiting doesn't get Kat in trouble. We've been apart for a while, and since I was in the area, I wanted to surprise her," he said with a jovial flair.

"I'm sorry," Derrick replied, "but who are you?"

"Ha, where are my manners? I'm Kat's boyfriend, Monty."

"Well, again, I'm sorry; she didn't mention she was dating." Derrick looked past him into the room. "Is Kat here?"

"No, I think she's downstairs. Please don't say anything just yet—I want to surprise her. I'll let her know you came by." Monty slowly closed the door with a smile.

Derrick just stood in front of the door frozen in place. *Boyfriend? Is she dating someone? This is too strange.* He walked back to his room and before stepping inside, looked back at her door, shaking his head. As his door closed, the elevator doors opened, and a clueless Kat stepped off and headed to her room.

She fumbled for her key card while balancing her ice bucket and a bottle of diet soda in her opposite arm. With the sound of the lock releasing, she pushed the door open with her foot and walked in, hearing the door click shut behind her. Setting the bucket on the dresser, she heard something else behind her, and turning, she found Monty stepping out of the dark bathroom. "Don't scream," he whispered, holding his index finger to his lips.

Chills quickly covered Kat's body, followed by the sensation of her feet submerged in concrete, and like a bad dream, her body shut down in fear. "I know we've had our differences, but I'm here to win you back. Please give me a chance." Monty placed his hands on her arms and rubbed up and down. The only movement from Kat was the shaking of her hands. "It will all work out," he whispered, placing his lips on her ear lobe.

With the flush of adrenaline beginning to flow through her body, she pushed back. "Monty, you need to leave," her voice shook.

"Baby, you don't really want me to leave," he said, taking a step toward her.

"Leave!" Her voice cracked with fear. Monty's grin slowly faded, a shade of red coming over his face, and he lunged toward her, catching her arms and gripping tight. She screamed again, but this time, it was followed with the palm of Monty's hand striking her right cheek and sending her to the floor at the foot of the bed.

Monty stood over her with his hand cocked to strike again, and she covered her head to shield the next blow. A loud explosion filled the room, stunning both her and her assailant, and the next sound she heard was the whoosh of breath leaving Monty's lungs and his body falling at her feet. She looked up to see Derrick reaching down to grab a handful of Monty's shirt and fling him out into the hall like a rag doll.

Derrick stepped out of the room toward Monty, who was cowardly hunched over against the wall. Derrick glanced at Kat, who was still in the same position, the fearful expression gradually leaving her face. Looking back to find Monty climbing to his feet with a hand protecting his face, Derrick threw a right hook, feeling his fist crack the left side of Monty's jaw. He was out before he hit the floor. Derrick rushed back into Kat's room and picked up the phone, dialing the front desk and ordering "Call 911. A young lady was attacked by a man." Derrick paused, "No, I knocked him out; he's in the hall. He's no threat right now."

Kat's arms were wrapped around Derrick when the police officers tightened the handcuffs on Monty, who still wasn't sure where he was. "Do we have to come to the police station?" Derrick asked.

"No, sir, I believe I have everything I need here," the officer said, pointing to his notebook, "and believe me, with a restraining order already on him, the judge won't let him see the light of day for a while. I have your number and will call if I need anything else. Don't hesitate to call us," he said to Kat.

"Thank you," she said in a soft tone.

"We will move you across the hall since the door jamb is broken," the hotel manager said to Kat. "And I know it doesn't help what has happened, but I will get to the bottom of this and find out how he got a key to your room."

"Here, let's pack your things," Derrick said, walking her back into her room.

Kat sat on the foot of her bed, and after fighting them back all evening, the tears started flowing. "I'm sorry, Derrick—I never thought he would track me down here. I've put everyone in danger." She covered her face, sobbing.

"Hey, it's not your fault. And I don't think anyone was in danger but you. Do you want to stay with me tonight? I can sleep on the floor."

She nodded yes, adding, "You don't have to sleep on the floor."

The officer returned to the room and knocked on the open door. "You said you guys were with Cedar Branch Community?"

"Yes, sir," Derrick answered.

"You guys let your folks go out on the town so late?"

"Well, we're not chaperones; we are really just trip leaders. Our guests are free to do what they want." Derrick looked down then back to the officer, "Out on the town?" he asked.

"My partner and I ran into a group of them at the Oyster Club earlier—just kinda strange for us."

"How far is the Oyster Club?" Kat asked.

"It's over in the southern district. Maybe 12 to 14 blocks from here. We saw them with a white van."

Derrick and Kat looked at each other, then walked to the window, looking out in the parking lot. "No, there's our van down there," Kat said, looking back at the officer.

"No worries. You folks get some rest," the officer said, walking toward the elevator doors. The light lit up, and with a ding from the elevator car, six retirees stepped out, trying to act innocent in front of the officers.

"Officers," Jack tipped his hat toward them.

"Sir," they greeted him and stepped into the elevator laughing, unaware of the white van in the parking lot with a chrome bumper still chained to the frame.

Chapter 42

During the night, Derrick was just what Kat expected, a true gentleman; he slept with one arm under her and pulling her close, giving her the one thing she needed—safety. Watching Derrick sleep, she lay on her side with her head propped up, allowing her hair to rain down the side of her arm onto the pillow. Thinking about her future and the closing of CBC, her thoughts drifted to the fact she could get fired for putting the group in danger and sleeping in the same room with Derrick.

She rolled over to her back, straightened her t-shirt, and taking a deep breath, she could see daylight trying to break through the curtains. The phone rang, causing her to jump with nerves shot. She lay still, trying to process the moment. Derrick rolled out of bed like a fireman waiting for the alarm. "Hello," he struggled to clear his throat. "A what? OK, give me a minute, and I'll be right down."

"What's the matter?" she asked.

"The front desk called to say that someone chained a bumper to our van." He ducked into the bathroom.

Walking back out, he found Kat sitting up with the TV on. "A bumper?" she questioned.

"I don't know, probably some kids playing a joke." He pulled a shirt over his head, and butterflies swirled in Kat's stomach looking at the six pack his abs showed. "I'll run down and look. Do you want me to bring you a coffee?"

"I better get back to my room before the group starts stirring. Do you think they took the van last night?"

"I don't know; Simon has the keys." He walked back into the bathroom to brush his teeth, adding, "They were acting rather peculiar last night, though."

"I'm sure everything will come out at breakfast," she replied.

He wiped his mouth with a cloth and walked out. "You OK?" he asked, and Kat gave his answer in a smile. He returned the smile and headed out. She fell back into the stack of pillows, sighing and not knowing what to think about last night.

After a few minutes, she collected her things and snuck out into the hallway barefooted, but before she could un-lock her door, she heard a snicker from behind her. She turned to find June in the hallway with her. "Oh, hi, June. I was just . . ."

June giggled and shrugged her shoulders, saying, "Your secret is safe with me."

"It's not really a secret, I mean, we aren't really... Oh, I don't know what I'm saying." Still scrambling for her words, Kat unlocked her door and disappeared inside. With her nerves still shot, she peeked into the bathroom and then under the beds. She could still feel Monty's cold hands touching her arms, but with Derrick nearby, she took a deep breath and stepped in the shower.

Jack and Gerald were sound asleep and unconsciously in competition for the loudest snore. A knock on their door grew louder before Jack woke up and opened the door to find Simon. "Hey, Mr. Goslin," Simon explained, "I didn't mean to wake you, but I am missing a backpack from the van. Have you seen it?"

"Yeah, hang on." Jack stumbled be into the dark room and returned with Simon's bag, adding, "Here are the keys, too."

"Did you guys take the van somewhere last night?" Simon questioned.

"I won't tell if you won't," Jack tapped the bag.

Simon gave a guilty grin. "Deal," he agreed, and left. Jack kept his balance with his hand on the wall and fell back into bed face first.

"Who was that?" Gerald mumbled.

"Our favorite pot head."

"Simon?" Gerald asked.

With a laugh, "Yep."

"Maybe we should get up and eat breakfast?"

"You go ahead," Jack pulled the sheets over his shoulder and closed his eyes. Before he could fall asleep, he heard Gerald snoring.

Out in the parking lot, Simon found Derrick and the hotel manager staring at the back of the van while one of the custodians removed the chrome bumper from the truck. "I'm not sure why someone would chain a bumper to the back of the van; it's not like we wouldn't have seen it before we drove off," Derrick said to the manager as Simon walked up. While Simon secretively laughed about knowing the truth, Derrick's phone buzzed with a text from Kat: "Getting a table for breakfast."

"That should do it," the custodian replied, pulling the bumper free.

"I am sorry for the practical joke," the manager said, looking at Derrick.

"Don't worry about it. You ready for breakfast?" he asked Simon, who gave a simple nod *yes*. They walked to the restaurant together in silence, not knowing both had secrets, one of dating Kat and the other tucked away in a backpack.

"I'll catch up with you—I need to head to the restroom first," Simon said, veering off in the lobby.

Derrick entered the restaurant to find Kat sitting alone at a table set for nine. "Where is everyone?"

"Your guess is as good as mine. I saw June this morning. Actually it was when I came out of your room," she hesitantly replied.

"Do you think she suspects anything?"

"Of course she does. Who are we kidding, they all know." She rolled her eyes.

"Well, let's keep it on the down low and we'll figure out something." He took a swig of his water.

"I don't know, Derrick. We are messing around with our jobs."

He could hear the concern rising in her voice. Gripping her hand and offering a warm smile, he assured her, "Trust me, we'll figure it out." The waitress returned to take orders, and without waiting on the group, the two of them ordered

216   Camp 80

breakfast. For the rest of the meal, they talked about every-thing but their predicament with work and dating and last night.

Chapter 43

One by one, everyone filed down the elevator to the lobby dragging their bags and their feet. While Violet argued about the order of the bags lined against the wall, Betty and June began planning their strategy on the morning shopping twenty feet below downtown Houston. Gerald was sitting in a seat, struggling to tie his new shoes, when Violet held her hand out in front of him. "Give me one of your shoes," she ordered.

Gerald slipped his right shoe off and handed it to her, and she quickly tied a bow, leaving enough slack in the laces to slip into them without having to retie them. "That's what I have to do with my shoes," she explained, handing them back.

He held his hand to the side of his mouth, hiding his words from Jack. "I miss my Velcro shoes."

"Underground!" Karl blurted out, startling everyone.

"It's a mall and offices," Betty replied.

"People in this world are just setting themselves up. If an earthquake hits, we'll all be buried alive."

"You afraid you're going to miss your funeral?" Violet asked.

Karl gave her a dirty look while Betty patted his arm. "You don't have to go; you and the other men could do something above ground."

"I'd like to stay above ground has long as possible, but I'm not letting you go down there without me," he whispered in Betty's ear.

Simon started grabbing bags to load into the van. "You guys ready?" Derrick asked. "I might have said this yesterday, but I want to remind everyone—"

Jack put his hand on Derrick's shoulder, saying, "Son, half of this group doesn't remember what you said this morning, much less yesterday."

"Well, we'll be at the mall in fifteen minutes or so, depending on traffic," he smiled.

Violet, June, and Gerald disappeared into the restroom with the news of the fifteen-minute ride. "It's just fifteen minutes," Derrick said out loud.

"Sweetheart, fifteen minutes is long enough," Betty replied.

Kat smiled at Betty. "Do you need to go?"

"No, I'm OK." Betty pulled her down closer, whispering, "At my age, what doesn't leak is dried up."

Kat covered her mouth to prevent laughing out loud. With Violet gone, Simon took the opportunity to quickly load the van. Once the bags were loaded, everyone wandered out of the restroom and started to climb in their seats for the drive to the mall. Violet had taken her stance at the side door of the van making sure no-one cheated on their seat when she heard her name being called, "Ms. Stevens!" A voice yelled. Turning to see who would be calling her by her last name she saw a gentleman dressed in uniform approaching her.

She shot a glance at June, "They've found us!"

"Found us?" June turned to see the sheriff of Camden, Arkansas walking up to the van.

"What do we do?" Violet asked with a terrified look. Everyone in the van remained silent in shock that the sheriff department was about to arrest the Stevens sisters.

"Don't over react!" June ordered her sister.

A smile formed on Karl's face, "This ought to be good."

The sisters frozen in place, "I'm glad I finally caught you." The sheriff stated with neither sister responding. He reached behind his back toward his handcuffs and pulled out a group of stapled papers folded in his back pocket, "I need both of your signatures to close the case." The tension in the air lifted.

"Signature?" Violet asked with a confused look.

"You're not going to arrest them?" Karl yelled from in the van.

"Why would I arrest them? It was just an accident, right?" He looked at Violet.

Shaking her head and looking down, "We've been meaning to fix that damn floor for nearly a year now."

"You mean you drove from Arkansas to Houston for a signature?" Karl asked, disappointed there wasn't going to be any drama.

"My daughter lives here, and it just gave me an excuse to get out of town." He watched both sisters sign the report and tipped his hat, saying, "Thank you, now I can head to see my grandkids. And don't worry about the cash you had in the room, it's safely locked in the station safe until you two can get back to properly put it in a bank."

"Thanks, Sheriff." Violet looked in the van, sticking her tongue out at Karl.

"Y'all have a great trip." He made his way back to his car.

Derrick looked at everyone with a halfcocked smile, "Well, everyone ready?" And once everyone was loaded, the van took off toward the underground mall. "Huh," Derrick said.

"What's the matter?" Simon asked.

"The van has a slight vibration in it."

Silence again covered the vehicle, and simultaneously everyone directed their attention out the windows. Derrick looked in the rear-view mirror at the reaction everyone had and the guilty expressions written on their faces. "Does anyone know about the bumper chained to the van?" Derrick asked.

"What bumper?" Jack blurted out.

"The one that was on our van this morning," Kat answered for Derrick.

"Is that why the police were at the hotel last night?" Violet changed the subject, not knowing she was bringing up a subject that Kat and Derrick didn't want to talk about.

"So where in the hell is this underground mall?" Karl yelled, changing the subject.

Everyone paused, looking at each other. "Underground," June affirmed. Everyone started laughing.

"I know it's underground, I mean where is the—Oh, never mind!" Karl grunted with his arms folded.

Everyone leaned with the turning of the van into a parking garage just off Main Street, and when Simon had put it in park, the group exited one by one. "Kat, do you want to come with us?" Betty asked.

"Where are you going?"

"Taking Violet for a make-over," Betty replied.

"A what!" Violet shot back.

"Oh, hush and come on." June took her by the arm, and Betty and Kat followed. Kat smiled at Derrick and gave a simple wave.

"That girl is smitten with you," Jack commented, putting his hand on Derrick's back.

"What?" Simon looked confused.

"We are just friends," Derrick replied. "Where to, men?"

"Increase my damn life insurance," Karl answered.

"Hey! Did you feel that?" Jack grabbed the side of the van.

Karl spun around with a startled expression. "What?" he snapped before he saw the devious grin growing on Jack's face. "Ass!" Karl spat out at him.

As the girls entered into the elevator, Kat noticed an advertisement describing 50% off on shoes at one of the stores. "I say we go there first. Look, they are also offering a free gift with each pair of shoes."

As the elevator doors began closing, Violet pointed out, "That's dumb! Aren't gifts supposed to be free?" The girls rolled their eyes at her comment.

As he walked across the parking lot with the other guys, Derrick's phone buzzed with a call from the director of Cedar Branch. "You guys go ahead; I'll catch up," he waved them on. "Good morning," he answered the call.

"Did you not think I'd find out?" The director's voice was raised.

"Find out what?" Derrick was caught off guard by the harsh comment, but quickly realized the call must be about him dating Kat. *We aren't really dating yet! And why would she call about this and not wait till we got back? Wait, last night! Kat stayed in my room, but who would have told or called the director?* Derrick was blown away.

"We have strict rules that we follow," the director sang back.

Why in the world is she so mad? "OK?" Derrick questioned.

"Well, explain?" she ordered.

"It just happened, OK? I didn't think it would go this far, but I don't agree with the rule about dating co-workers," Derrick defended himself.

A long pause on the other line. "What *are* you talking about?"

"Kat and myself."

"You two are *dating*?"

"Isn't that what you're talking about?" Derrick questioned.

"I'm talking about Kat's ex-fiancé in her room and being arrested. My rule is you let me know immediately if something happens that puts anyone in jeopardy. But I guess you have more explaining to do."

Derrick lowered the phone and closed his eyes, muttering "Crap!"

Chapter 44

Derrick had remained quiet walking with the men throughout their walk through the mall, not noticing the shoppers shuffling their way around the slow group. He had made many mistakes in his career, but pulling Kat into his biggest mistake had his stomach churning. Jack and Karl were oblivious to his silence, but when he missed a few funny comments, Gerald had picked up that something was wrong.

After Jack and Karl found the restroom and disappeared inside, Gerald turned to Derrick, saying, "What's the matter? You've been quiet this whole time."

"Nothing, just got a few things on my mind. Thanks for asking," he politely smiled.

"I know I don't say much and seem docile, but I know when something is bothering people. Want to talk?" Gerald smiled back.

Something about Gerald's soft demeanor pulled Derrick into confiding with him. "The director knows about Kat and myself. They have strict rules." He paused and looked at Gerald. "I really do like her, but I can't be the cause for the end of her career."

"I'm sure the director is professional enough to handle your relationship in a healthy manner. And I'm sure you two aren't the first."

"Well, there's more to it. Last night, the police were at the hotel for an incident that happened between Kat and her ex-boyfriend." Derrick looked at his phone to check the time. "Turns out he had been stalking her, and last night he was waiting for her in her room. If I hadn't been there, then something bad could have happened. Anyway, it could have put everyone in danger, so I think the director is more concerned about what Kat's relationships have done."

"Wow, didn't know that. You guys are good at hiding your emotions."

"I'm sure we'll have some changes when we get back." Derrick put his hand on Gerald's shoulder, adding, "But I don't need to worry about this. Whatcha say we gather this gang and head to lunch?"

"Sounds good, but I'm here if you need an ear," Gerald smiled.

Karl and Jack came out of the bathroom with Karl griping, "I'm telling you, those hot air hand blowers blow nothing but bathroom germs on your hand!" Karl shouted above the crowd in the mall.

With a perturbed expression, Jack scrolled through his phone, not paying any attention to Karl, and reaching Derrick, he handed him his phone. "My son texted me, and I can't figure out where it went. Why he has to text and not call, I don't know."

"Kids don't have a clue what social life is now-a-days," Karl grumbled, changing his gripe to texting.

Before long, the ladies came into view, carrying shopping bags, eating ice cream, and talking. "Look at that," Karl said. "All four of them talking and no one listening."

"What did you say, Karl?" Jack smiled.

"I said... ." He noticed Jack was messing with him. "Ass!"

"For a religious man, you sure use the word *ass* a lot."

"First, I'm not all religious, and second *ass* is not a bad word. It's in the Bible," Karl defended himself.

"I don't think it's in the Bible with the context you use it," Gerald piped up.

Karl stopped and looked at them. "You mean to tell me that you guys, including Mr. Encyclopedia"—he pointed to Gerald—"haven't heard the miracle of stretching skin in Exodus?"

The four men looked at each other, then back at Karl. "I guess we haven't," Gerald answered for them.

"In Exodus, Moses tied his ass to a tree and walked forty miles!" Karl smiled.

The men exploded into laughter, the women hesitating to walk up in fear they were laughing at them. "What's so funny?" Kat asked.

"Karl," Jack laughed and explained the remark.

Within an hour, the group was loaded back in the van with Violet's new wardrobe and speeding toward the Aquarium restaurant. Betty kept hinting to the men to compliment Violet on her hair and outfit, but none of the men understood what she was trying to imply. Stepping out of the van in the parking lot, Betty whispered to Karl, "Tell Violet she looks nice."

"Why?" He blurted out.

"Shhh, because it's polite."

"Why do I have to? Get Jack, he's all about the ladies."

"Karl," Betty's voice grew.

Karl leaned behind Betty while walking to the restaurant. "You look nice," he said in an unconvincing tone.

"Thank you," Violet smiled, then turned to Betty. "Thank *you*," she grinned.

June led the group into the lobby of the restaurant and suddenly stopped, gazing about the colossal area surrounded with aquariums ranging from salt water to fresh water. The deep blue lighting set the atmosphere and tone for an underwater experience and tranquil vibe. Karl walked into June's back with his eyes running about the restaurant, followed by Betty and the rest of the group.

Kat smiled at the hostess. "Table for nine, please."

"Let me check," she smiled back and ran her finger across the seating chart behind the podium.

Two ladies were leaving the dining area when one of them smiled at Jack and softly said "Hi." Jack tipped his hat toward her and gave a gentlemanly grin back, then turned to Karl, saying, "I'm liking Texas more and more."

"I don't think it matters what state the hen house is in, just as long as it has chicks," Karl replied, covering his mouth for only Jack to hear.

Jack shook his head. "Karl, you are astounding me more and more," he laughed.

"Right this way," the young hostess said with a smile. The group followed, running into chairs and tables as they gazed around at the décor of the dining area.

Violet ran into a man sitting in his chair, causing food to fall off his fork. He turned with an annoyed expression, but Gerald interrupted with "Sorry, she just killed her attorney."

The man looked at his wife sitting at the table. "What did he say?"

"She just came from a funeral?" the man's wife replied, not hearing Gerald clearly.

After everyone was seated, and the waiter had taken their drink orders, Violet piped up with "What's on the schedule for today?"

"After lunch," Kat answered as the waiter returned with their drinks, "we are heading to the beach, and all our rooms face the ocean."

"Can I take your orders?" the waiter asked.

One by one, everyone questioned everything on the menu from lunch to dinner options. When it came time for Karl to order, he handed his menu to the young man, saying, "I'll have the grilled chicken with fries."

"Chicken? We're at a seafood restaurant," Jack said.

"So? There's no rule about ordering."

"It's like going to a Mexican place and ordering Italian," June replied.

"And that's like saying a football player can only play football. I'll have the chicken," Karl insisted, staring at the waiter.

"Yes, sir," the waiter replied.

Chapter 45

Gerald was staring out the window watching downtown Houston grow smaller and the Gulf of Mexico grow larger. Jack sat beside him in a showdown with Karl over the government and the hormones given to chickens, a debate that Gerald thought was funny; he wondered who had more hot air. Unknown to everyone in the van, this particular day marked the eighth month since Gerald's wife had passed. Gripped in his right hand was a picture that he secretly kept in the pocket of his Members Only jacket.

"What do you think?" Jack turned to Gerald.

"About what?" Gerald was clueless about the question or what part of the debate they were in.

"Exactly, Gerald. Useless to even talk about it," Violet piped up from the seat in front of him.

"You're not helping me," Jack playfully replied.

"I'm sorry—my mind was drifting."

"Kat," Karl started, "why are we driving six hours to

the beach when Cedar Branch is less than thirty minutes away?"

"It's not about the beach. It's about us being together," Betty answered for Kat.

"We live together! Or we will."

"Is there somewhere else you'd rather go?" Kat smiled.

"Nah, I guess I'm more worried about Violet and that bathing suit."

Betty popped him on the side. "What's wrong with my bathing suit?" Violet asked.

"It shows more than I want to see."

"Karl! Don't be rude," Betty said, turning red.

"Well, I admire that you have the courage to wear it," Kat chimed in, trying to soften the air.

"Courage?" Karl started again, but received a sharper punch from Betty.

"I'm 83 and figure I'll be dead soon," replied Violet with a smile, "so I might as well live."

"Keep wearing that and we'll all be dead," Karl said under his breath.

They barreled down interstate 45 heading south with salt air drifting through the vents into the van. A blue four-door truck flew past them missing a back bumper, but nobody noticed until Derrick made a comment about the missing appendage. Everyone broke out into mad laughter, leaving Derrick to think that it wasn't that funny, so he must be missing something.

"Ladies, why did you never marry?" Jack changed the subject.

Violet turned in her seat. "You asking?"

"You wearing that bathing suit today?" he smiled back.

"I would say a lot had to do with our father dying and us seeing our mom so miserable," June spoke up.

"For me, I'm just waiting on the right guy," Violet shouted above her sister.

"How did your father die?" Betty asked.

"It was the war," June started.

"Civil war?" Karl snickered.

"Haha, you're only one year younger." June replied, sitting up. "The second war, we were young, but still remember seeing mama on the old wooden floor of our house screaming. It was a picture that I could never forget. And I don't know—I just thought there was nothing worse than having that happen to me. So I never married."

"Did you ever date?" Betty pushed for more information.

"Oh yea, Daniel Burkenstein!" June said with a smile. He was the prettiest boy I ever met."

"And you would have married him if he hadn't enlisted in the Army," Violet broke in her story.

"Maybe, but he never did come back either," June replied with a look at her sister.

"You three don't know how good you have it; times were tough back then," Karl said to Simon, Derrick, and Kat.

"Oh, I don't know, I think we've lived in the best era," Jack said.

"What world are you living in?" Karl shot back.

"I know we've seen our share of wars, but everyone has. There was no better time than the 50's and the turn of the new age after the second war. Hell, we lived when baseball was a pastime, not just a sport."

A car slid into the lane of the van, causing Derrick to brake and sending everyone forward bracing themselves. "Jerk!" Derrick yelled. "Sorry, guys."

"Speaking of jerks, is that stalker ex-boyfriend going to stay in jail?" Violet asked Kat.

Feeling her stomach drop, Kat froze before answering the question; she thought they had kept it under wraps. She looked at June, who shrugged her shoulders. "I didn't say anything—they already knew."

"Yeah, what's the story there? And why haven't you said anything?" Karl asked. Normally, Betty would punch him and say it wasn't his business, but she just sat smiling at Kat, waiting for the gossip.

"I'm sorry, guys. I didn't want to worry you about it," Kat started.

"She's worried about putting everyone in harm's way," Derrick interjected.

"Harm's way? We're all gonna be dead soon anyways!" Karl blurted out.

"Speak for yourself," Jack said and looked back at Kat.

Everyone else had kept their attention on Kat. "I dated him in college, and after a couple of years he became very possessive and demanding. I broke it off with him, and it got worse, to the point I had to get a restraining order on him. He just turned into a nightmare with stalking and calling, even after the restraining order. I haven't heard from him in a long time and figured it was over, but I guess I was wrong." She lowered her head.

"Sweetie, you hang around us, and he'll never bother you." Violet held her purse up and patted it.

"What are you going to do? Mace him to death?" Karl chuckled.

"Mace? Mace is for wimps." Violet reached in her purse and pulled out a nickel-plated Smith and Wesson .357 with wooden grips.

"Good Lord!" Karl yelled. Everyone in the van gasped for air and Derrick accidentally swerved into another lane looking in the rearview mirror. "Is that loaded?"

Violet gave him a funny look. "What do you think? Of course it's loaded. What good is an unloaded gun?"

"You've been carrying that this whole time?" Jack asked.

Turning in her seat, Violet answered, "Never leave home without it." She smiled.

"I take back anything I said about your bathing suit," Jack grinned.

"Hell, I take back everything," Karl gulped.

"Oh, it's too late for you," Violet smiled at Karl, giving him the same sinking feeling Kat had.

"Are you packing too?" Karl asked June.

With a sly grin, June replied, "Piss me off and find out." Everyone in the van laughed except Karl.

Karl whispered to Betty, "What floor are they moving to in our building?"

Chapter 46

Pulling to a stop, Derrick turned to everyone in the van, saying "Welcome to your beach front getaway."

The group looked through the windshield at two light blue cottages that stood only feet apart from each other. A small white picket fence lined the yard with a cobblestone walkway leading to the beach running between the two cozy cottages. Simon stepped out and opened the door for Kat and the others.

"How is this going to work?" Karl lifted an eyebrow at Kat.

"Boys in one cabin and girls in another," She said, looking back at him and holding back a smile.

Karl looked at Betty, then back at Kat. "What?" His voice grew louder.

"I'm kidding. There are separate rooms you can choose from," Kat grinned.

Violet pushed her way through everyone and bolted toward the beach without saying anything, Jack laughed at her persistence and followed behind her. One by one, everyone strolled down the path heading to the water, leaving Simon with a van load of luggage. As they walked onto the brown sandy beach, a south wind greeted them with the warmth left over from the day. The sun was tracking on its daily path, soon to disappear into the Gulf of Mexico.

"I think our beach is prettier," Karl grumbled.

"The ocean stirs the heart, inspires the imagination and brings eternal joy to the soul," Gerald spoke, gazing out into the ocean with the wind blowing what little hair he had.

Karl shot him a glance. "Robert Wyland."

Gerald smiled back. "You know the artist?"

Karl looked back out at the waves crashing on the beach. "I do."

June was the first to slip out of her flats and walk barefooted into the water, the cool salt water quickly burying her feet into the sand. Jack kicked off his shoes and rolled up his pants, following June into the water. Once ankle deep, he looked up and spotted a structure in the distance. "I see where I am ending up."

The group turned their attention to the beach side bar only a few doors down from their cottages. "Actually, that is where we are eating tonight, so we'll all be joining you," Kat replied.

"I better help Simon so he doesn't shoot himself in the leg carrying my bags," Violet walked past everyone.

"How many guns did you bring?" Karl asked with wide eyes.

"Do you really want to know?" she grinned.

With a smile, he admitted, "Not really."

Everyone started back to the van to grab their bags and pick out a room for the next two nights. Jack snatched his shoes and started to follow, but stopped shy of Gerald, who was still in a trance staring into the depths of the gulf. He turned and stood next to Gerald. "It's always a majestic sight."

Gerald remained speechless and nodded his head in acknowledgment. Jack took it as a hint to give him a moment alone. After a few steps, he heard Gerald speak up, "Eight months today."

Jack walked back. "Doris?"

Gerald nodded again. "I am sorry," Jack replied. "I'd be lying if I said I know how you feel."

"It's OK. I'll be with her again someday." He smiled at Jack and headed back to the cottages. Jack trailed behind, thinking that if losing someone to death was half as hard as losing them to divorce, it was something he wasn't sure he wanted to know.

Once at the cottage, Jack and Gerald found that Simon had taken in their bags to the cottage that Karl and Betty had settled in. The interior was decorated with white-washed walls and dark plank wooden floors. Betty and Karl were in the living room. "Kat said we are eating in thirty minutes at the Crab Shaq down the street," Betty told the men as they entered the room.

"That doesn't give me much time before we eat," Jack replied.

"For what?" Karl asked.

"My pre-dinner drink." Jack turned to Gerald, "Want to join me?"

"Sure," Gerald replied, and together the two walked to

the bar and grill. The street was barricaded with orange cones and barrels as a construction crew worked late into the evening finishing pouring new curbs on the street. Jack tipped his hat at the young men as they poured concrete while a big husky man supervised the progress.

"You're going to miss happy hour," Jack said to the big man, pointing to his watch.

"Might have to today, gotta finish this street," the man replied, never changing expressions.

Jack and Gerald were welcomed by a young hostess. "Table?" she asked.

"Not yet," Jack replied, pointing instead to the bar, which was empty but for a dark-complexioned bartender standing behind the rose cherry bar.

"What'll it be, gentlemen?" the bartender asked.

"Bourbon," Jack said, dropping his hat on the bar.

Betty and Karl walked over to the next cottage to find Derrick and Simon waiting on Kat, June, and Violet. "You guys coming?" Karl yelled through the small cottage.

Kat ducked her head out of a room, "You guys go ahead; we'll be right behind you." The four of them walked out and down the same path Jack and Gerald had taken. The wind had picked up from the coast, giving the construction crew relief from a sun that was starting its descent into the ocean.

Violet, who was now standing in the living room, yelled back to the room, "Y'all ready?" June walked out, followed by Kat, who was wearing a light blue and yellow sundress. "He should like that," Violet replied.

Kat shook her head. "I think Derrick and I have let our feelings for each other become too well known."

"If you like someone, you shouldn't let any job tell you what to do," Violet snapped back.

"Plus we're good at keeping secrets," June smiled. Violet laughed, making Kat uncomfortable about keeping secrets.

The three of them headed out down the street toward the Crab Shaq. A strong wind blew through the cottages, stirring up a small cloud of sand and causing everyone to cover their eyes. Getting closer to the restaurant, the construction crew took notice of Kat and the small sundress that defined every curve on her body. The husky man yelled at his men to get back to work and stop gawking at the woman. He smiled and tipped his hardhat as if he were keeping the young men at bay.

Another strong wind quickly blew through the street, catching everyone by surprise, including Kat, who raised her hands to cover her eyes while the wind lifted something else—her cute little sundress, revealing her legs and the light blue pair of panties she was wearing under the dress. Kat quickly dropped her arms and pulled her dress down to find the construction crew frozen motionless as if a wish had come true. "Shit!" Kat exclaimed with horrified glance back at the crew, who were now clapping. "Oh, my gosh, how embarrassing!" She turned red and stepped in front of June to hide from the happy stares.

June gently patted her back, saying, "Don't sweat it, sweetie. At least they clapped for you—at my age they just gasp for air!"

Chapter 47

Kat sat beside Simon at the table, still red from the incident outside, and with shaking hands took a gulp from the water sitting in front of her. Derrick watched as she struggled with the glass. "Are you OK?" he asked.

She held up her free hand toward him and nodded with the glass still resting on her lips. "She's fine—she just gave the construction workers a show they won't forget," Violet replied, flipping out her napkin and seating it in her lap. Kat choked and spit the water in her mouth back into the glass, spraying part of the table. Everyone jumped, then just stared, anticipating her story.

"Thanks, Violet." Kat wiped her mouth.

"No problem."

"The wind blew up my dress a little while walking down the street. Just embarrassed me, that's all," she told Derrick.

"A little! More like blew your dress up to your face showing those cute baby blue panties," Violet announced.

Kat sank in her chair wishing she was dead; she bit her bottom lip and glanced over at Derrick, praying he hadn't heard Violet, but with his snickering, she knew better.

"I wouldn't worry about it—you probably gave those men just the right amount of energy to finish their job," Jack said, holding up his glass.

"You know she's probably—" Violet started.

"OK, enough about Kat's show. You guys are embarrassing her more. Let's change the subject," Betty said.

Everyone turned their focus on the menu and studied it until the waitress walked up with a pad and pen, but after she realized no one was paying her any attention, she said she would give them a moment or two. Kat looked back at Derrick, who gave her a gentleman's smile, comforting her a little after Violet's announcement of the color of her panties.

"Guys, I'm not very hungry, so if you don't mind, I am excusing myself for a walk on the beach," Gerald said quietly, setting his menu down.

"Are you OK?" Kat asked.

"Yeah, I'm fine. Just not hungry. I'll catch you guys back at the cottages." He pushed his chair back under the table and walked through the bar area and down the steps onto the sand.

"Today marked the eighth month since Doris's death," Jack spoke up.

"Oh no—maybe you should go check on him," Betty said, elbowing Karl.

Before Karl could say anything, Jack answered, "He needs time alone."

Their table sat next to a large window giving them a front row seat to the beach, ocean, and the finishing sunset that had painted the sky a bright fire orange. Jack watched as Gerald slowly walked toward their cottages, watching the seagulls play in the surf and looking for their next meal. Something made Jack feel uneasy about Gerald's strange demeanor; he was always quiet, but there was something about this time that made Jack feel sorry for him. Jack's separations from his wives had been chosen by either him or his wives, something he had a little control over. But for Gerald's loss, he couldn't wrap his head around a separation that was uncontrollable.

After eating, the group sat at the table trading stories about family and funny experiences they had within the last year. Betty stretched her arms and looked at Karl, saying, "I am tired. I might head back and turn in early tonight."

"OK." Karl started to get up.

"No, you stay."

"I'm not going to let you walk back by yourself," Karl said.

"We're heading back also, so we'll walk with her and make sure those construction workers don't gawk at her," June laughed.

"Oh, I don't know, maybe I can flip up my dress to give them a show," Betty laughed, pushing on Kat's shoulders.

"Thanks," Kat smiled.

"They're gone anyway," Simon commented, walking back in the front door from a phone call.

Kat stood up. "I'm heading back while I'll can." Everyone headed for the door except Karl and Jack, who decided to order drinks to go and walk the beach back. Jack wanted to check with Gerald.

The beach was lit by a few street lights, and the quarter moon that was peeking over the horizon of the Gulf. The men walked through the light brown sand toward the water to walk back on wet sand. "What made you want to hang back with me tonight?" Jack asked, sipping on his bourbon.

"I need some air and to check on Gerald. Ever since Kat has been helping with our meds, I seem to feel better. I think my wife was drugging me."

"She might have been planning to knock you off early to enjoy a younger man with your money," Jack laughed.

"I don't know about a younger man, but I know money isn't it. I don't have any," he laughed back. In the distance, they could see the figure of someone sitting on the beach facing the ocean. "That looks like our boy," Karl said, thinking it was Gerald.

"He's not taking today very well," Jack replied.

"Hell, neither would I." They slowly walked in the direction of the person relaxing in the sand after watching a remarkable sunset. It was Gerald leaning back against a lounge chair that one of the cottages had left out. Walking closer, Karl spoke loud enough for him to hear. "You missed a good supper, but I guess you had a better view of the sunset out here."

Jack looked at Karl. "I don't think he heard you."

"Don't tell me you're getting hard of hearing too," Karl called with a smile.

Gerald didn't move; he seemed to be focused on the rolling waves working their way up the beach. Jack reached down and touched his knee. "Hey?" he asked. Gerald didn't answer. Jack looked at Karl, then back at Gerald. "Gerald?"

He shook his knee. Gerald's right hand fell to the sand, opening and releasing the picture of Doris. "Gerald!" Jack's voice grew.

Karl put his hand on Jack's shoulder. "Jack," he said, his voice quiet.

Jack knelt beside Gerald and looked in his partially open eyes, then shook his head in agreement with Karl's perception of the situation. "You son-of-a-bitch," Jack said, then looked up at Karl. "Eight months apart. I guess that was as long as he wanted to go." Jack turned back to Gerald and gently closed his eyes with his left hand. "You're with her now," he said quietly, a happy tear beginning to blur his vision.

"I need to go get Derrick," Karl said.

"Wait." Jack moved down to Gerald's new shoes, untied as usual. As he tied them for the last time, "I envy you," he whispered to Gerald.

Chapter 48

The lights from the emergency vehicles reflected off the windows from the cottages that faced the beach. A small crowd formed on the back porch of the Crab Shaq to see what was taking place on the beach. Derrick stood with Jack and Karl as the paramedics placed Gerald on a stretcher covered with a white sheet. A paramedic walked up with a clipboard and pen in hand. "Did Mr. Harriman have a history of heart problems?" he asked Derrick.

"No, his medical file was clean. He seemed to be in good health."

"Nothing recent to indicate chest pains or shortness of breath?"

Derrick looked at Jack, "No, he was just down that today marked the eighth month since his wife passed away," Jack replied.

"Died of a broken heart," Karl said.

"I'm sure the coroner will have you fill out some paperwork to have the body sent to his family." The paramedic handed Derrick a stack of papers with a number written on the front page. "Call me if you need anything."

With papers in hand, "I will," Derrick answered.

The three men walked back to the cottage where Kat and Simon were sitting with the others. Everyone just stared with blank expressions and mixed emotions. Karl wrapped his arm around Betty and drew her close. "Do we need to call his family?" June asked.

"No, the director normally makes those calls." Derrick looked at Kat. "I better call her." He walked inside. Everyone sat outside on the deck watching the last of the emergency vehicles drive off the beach. Once the engines faded off into the streets, the sounds of the waves crashing on the sand returned.

"This is weird—I feel like we should be doing something?" June said.

"I never know what to say during times like this," Betty replied.

"Not much you can say except he is happy now." Karl pulled Betty tight with his arm still around her.

Violet cleared her throat. "This is the weird part for me because I don't believe in the hereafter."

Karl looked at her with a cocked eyebrow. "What do you believe?"

"Nothing."

"You can't believe that Gerald is just nowhere?" Karl questioned.

"I don't know what I believe in," she answered as Derrick walked back out onto the deck.

"The director is taking the first flight in the morning for here," Derrick said, looking at everyone and then to Kat. "Can I speak with you for a moment?" He waved her into the cottage. She walked in, leaving everyone in a sober mood. Simon gathered firewood from a rack to light a fire in the fire pit that centered the deck.

The rest of the evening, everyone sat around the fire talking about Gerald and their own lives, and for the first time, Jack became the quiet one of the group. Karl asked a few times if he was all right, but Jack answered he was fine, knowing that he wasn't.

The following morning before everyone was up, Kat met Derrick out front next to the van carrying her bags. "You ready?" Derrick asked in a sober tone.

"Yeah." She climbed in the front seat of the van to head to the airport to meet the director and catch a flight back to Cedar Branch. Neither said much, wondering what the director had in store for them and wondering what each other thought.

Parking into short-term parking, Derrick helped Kat with her bags. "I'm not sure why the director is taking your place for the last day," he said, looking at her.

"She is just doing her job. If I were the director and I had lost someone on a trip, I'd join the trip too," Kat responded, trying to make sense of the situation.

They were greeted by the director while standing in line to get Kat's ticket. "Once you get your ticket," she said to both of them, "let's talk." She pointed to a cluster of couches in front of a coffee shop.

Derrick and Kat joined her with Kat's ticket in hand. "You two have had a unique trip so far," the director started.

"You can say that," Derrick sat on one of the couches.

"And as I expected, you two handled everything professionally and to the best interest of our retirees." She gave Kat a short sense of relief until she followed up with, "But both of you have been extremely unprofessional with the rules of Cedar Branch. These rules about dating are set in place for very good reasons." Kat felt her stomach turn.

"I made mention of us, but we have not in the least bit allowed it to interfere with our job," Derrick replied, growing defensive.

The director looked at Derrick. "Your relationship is the number-one topic on this orientation trip, according to Simon." Derrick and Kat looked at each other, thinking the same thought: Simon? "But he didn't sell you out—he simply answered a hard question I asked." she continued.

"I never—" Kat started, but was interrupted by the director.

"This is hard for me and in some way makes no sense with the possibility of Cedar Branch closing, but I have no choice except to let both of you go." She reached in her bag and pulled a pink-colored slip of paper out and handed it to each of them. "Derrick, you will receive pay until we get back, and Kat, well, today is your last day."

"You're bribing me to finish the trip?" Derrick asked.

"Professionally, I expect nothing less." She cut her eyes at him.

Derrick shot up, "I will not—" but Kat pulled him back down.

"Keep Derrick; you'd be a fool not to. You will need his help closing Cedar Branch." She handed the pink slip back. "I pursued Derrick for a relationship, so it wasn't his fault.

I have a clever way of manipulating people. I quit!" Kat stood up with tears building.

Derrick stood back up, knowing she was lying about being manipulating. "Kat, you—"

She held up her hand. "Goodbye." She turned toward her gate, leaving the director and Derrick confused.

Derrick started after her. "Let her go," the director said in a calm voice.

He shot a go-to-hell look back at her, "I am not going to let you get away with this."

"Derrick." The director stood up. "She is only doing what I ask." Derrick's expression went from rage to confusion. "I have a director's job lined up for you in a neighboring retirement community. The only way I can give you a written recommendation is if Kat confesses to leading you on and quits."

"What?"

"She quit for you." Derrick watched Kat walk up the stairs and vanish into the terminal, and then he looked back at the director. "Trust me," she added.

Chapter 49

Derrick remained quiet on the way back to the cottage. Getting no responses to his text messages to Kat, he hoped it was because she was already on the plane heading back. The director tried to explain further into her plan to save Derrick's career, but felt he was more emotional over Kat and decided to stay quiet.

Putting the van in park, he climbed out and headed to his cottage, "Kat's room was in that cabin. I'll make sure everyone is up and we can meet in a few for you to explain what's going on."

"I am only going to talk about the trip and explain that Kat has gone home early. I don't want to upset anyone about her losing her job," the director explained.

"They're not idiots—they will know." Derrick disappeared into his cottage.

Twenty minutes later, everyone gathered in the living room of Derrick's cottage to meet and then head to breakfast. The coffee maker was on its second pot with Karl already setting up for a third.

"I know last night was probably a long night," the director started.

"Where's Kat?" Betty asked.

"She has gone home early."

"Did you fire her?" Betty interrupted her.

Before the director could address the comment, Karl spoke up, "Why in the hell did she lose her job? It's tough enough that we lost Gerald last night."

The director quickly realized that maybe her decision to send Kat home might be backfiring. She looked at Derrick for help, but didn't receive any. "My job is not the easiest, and many times I don't make the best decisions, but I felt it was best that Kat head home early and let me fill in to help finish the trip."

"This trip was over at eight o'clock last night." Jack sipped on his coffee.

"Well, that is my question, Do you guys want to finish the trip or... ."

"I'm done," Violet shouted from the back.

"Me too," Karl agreed.

"I have Gerald's things packed. I'd rather head back to Cedar Branch and start unpacking my apartment." Jack stood up.

Without the director having to say anything else, everyone headed to their rooms to pack and make the eight-hour trip back to Cedar Branch. With everyone's mixed emotions on Gerald's death and Kat's dismissal, Derrick decided it would be best to drive through somewhere for breakfast and make lunch in Louisiana.

Standing at the back of the van, Simon looked at Violet for her normal instructions on loading bags. "Just throw the damn things in and let's go," she said and climbed in the side door. A depressing vibe lurked over the group as they headed out of Galveston Beach, a place none of them would ever return.

After stopping for gas and a restroom break, the director asked Derrick if he would like for her to drive, and for the first time on the trip, Derrick gave up the wheel with no argument. He sat in the passenger seat staring out as the Texas scenery flashed by. He phone buzzed with a text from Kat.

The message read, *"I'm sorry this was all my fault. I would like to talk but I think it would be best if I took a few weeks to gather my thoughts."*

"I am confused. Why did you quit?" Derrick texted back.

"The director explained that if you were fired, she wouldn't be able to write the recommendation for you to get the other director job. You deserve it and will make a great director."

"Let me decide that. Don't you think this is a little over dramatic?"

"Yes, but if I didn't quit, we'd both be fired."

"What about us?"

"I have too much baggage."

"Something I'm willing to take," Derrick replied, but his screen stayed blank.

Jack sat in the back seat quiet and sober; he wanted to stretch out, but felt funny about taking part of Gerald's seat. He pulled out his phone and managed to get to his pictures for the first time by himself. He flipped through pictures of Karl, Gerald, and himself buying shoes. He tried to text Kat a message that he had figured out his phone, but couldn't find her number in the contacts. Frustrated, he set it in the seat and drifted away.

Betty clung to Karl's hand and gave him a smile, a smile he thought would last forever, but with more wrinkles appearing, a fear came over him that she might die before him, something he didn't want.

Chapter 50

After a few days back at Cedar Branch, Derrick walked to the independent living apartments to see if Karl and Betty needed help with anything moving in. He still strongly disagreed with the board of trustees' decision to remain quiet about the home declaring bankruptcy. Derrick had thought about sharing the news with the group from the trip, but in fear of losing his next job, kept it under the table.

Karl was sitting in the lobby reading a paper. "Hi, Karl. What are you doing down here? Aren't you guys moving in?" Derrick asked.

Folding the paper down and looking at Derrick over his reading glasses, Karl grumbled, "The boss said that my blood pressure would be better if I stayed down here out of the way."

Derrick sat beside him, "You seem to be handling it well."

"What?"

"The stress of moving in," Derrick replied.

"I don't stress."

Derrick chuckled under his breath. "Have you seen Jack?"

"Mr. Single? Or should I say, Mr. Cedar Branch?"

"Why do you say that?" Derrick laughed.

"He's like a lone rooster in a hen house." Karl pointed outside at Jack, who was standing in front of an umbrella table surrounded by ladies, all widows.

"Are you guys hanging out?"

"With Jack? Why in the hell would I want to hang out with him?"

"Oh, I don't know. Maybe because you're neighbors."

Before Karl had a chance to answer, the door swung open, with Jack wearing his typical fedora hat and white slacks. "Hello, Charming," Jack slapped Derrick on the back.

"You seem to be fitting in well," Derrick gave him a smile.

Bending down closer to Derrick's ear, Jack said, "I'd moved in here years ago if I had known all these eligible dames were here." Looking up at Karl, he said, "We still on for supper and my balcony for bourbon and cigars tonight?"

"Yep," Karl answered, grinning at Derrick.

"Have you talked to Kat?" Jack asked.

"I've tried texting a few times, but no answer. She wanted space and time."

"Do you not read books or watch movies? Girls want to be chased; you need to go find her." Jack waved him to the door.

"I don't know," Derrick said while his phone buzzed with a message from the director asking him to meet in her office. "Well, the boss is calling." He held up his phone.

Jack sat in his place. "Take my advice," he yelled at Derrick, who was walking out, and gave him a wave back over his shoulder. Jack turned to Karl. "They're still moving you in?"

Karl went back to his paper. "Yep."

Jack gripped the arms of his chair, saying, "I think I'll go check on the Stevens Sisters and see if Violet needs help getting in that two-piece bikini of hers." Karl cringed and shook at the same time at a thought he didn't want to imagine again.

"See you tonight!" The door shut behind him.

Derrick walked through the park and checked on the fountain that had been down for the last week. With a smirk, he watched it spewing out water, then stopping, then starting again. An elderly man sitting nearby reading a book said, "Looks like me when I'm peeing." The old man grinned at Derrick.

"I'll call them back to work on it," he said and then headed to the main office. Once he turned the corner to the last stretch of sidewalk to the office, he noticed a group of well-dressed people leaving the building. His head dropped at the thought of the visitors being lawyers delivering the papers of bankruptcy and the final blow to Cedar Branch. He noticed two of the members of the board walking with them laughing and carrying on, something that made his blood boil. *Laughing? What a bunch of jerks!*

He slung open the door and marched to the director's office. He had opened up more to venting with her since they had been back. The director was standing behind her desk. "Sit," she said. "I'll be right back." She hurried out and spoke to her assistant and returned.

Derrick looked at her expression, which was cheerful, with a funny look. "Why so happy? And why did the board members leave laughing? Not the best of times around here."

"It is now," she grinned.

"What?"

"That happened to be a group of attorneys that left with the board members."

"I figured that much."

"Not what you think." She shut the door, then sat beside Derrick. "That was Gerald Harriman's attorneys—the ones who are overseeing his estate."

"Okay?"

"Gerald didn't want anyone to know, but he was wealthy. Extremely wealthy. He is a direct heir to the Vanderbilts, and … well … someone told him that Cedar Branch was in financial trouble." She raised an eyebrow at him.

"I didn't," Derrick defended himself.

"I know. Kat did. So he called while on the orientation trip and set up a corporation to buy Cedar Branch. In the quick process, he asked his attorneys to change his will in case he passed away and couldn't buy it. Kind of weird—it was like he knew."

"So?"

"He left Cedar Branch twenty-eight million dollars," she grinned.

"So Cedar Branch isn't closing?"

"I'd say not."

"But I have already accepted the director's position at the other retirement community," Derrick replied.

"That is your decision if you want to continue that route; however, I will offer you the assistant director position here and match their pay. I am retiring next year, and the board would like for you to take over this seat."

"Wow." His mind was spinning.

"There is just one request that we have to fulfill in accepting the money."

"What's that?"

"That we build a fine arts center."

"OK, that's not a big deal."

"The condition is that we hire someone who is passionate about art and qualified."

"OK?" Derrick wasn't sure why she was making a big deal out of the request. A light knock came from the closed door.

The director stood up and grabbed the doorknob. "I believe you might know who I am talking about. Gerald was very specific in his request." She opened the door for Kat, who was standing on the other side.

"Hey," she said softly to Derrick, biting her bottom lip.

Chapter 51

Sitting on Jack's balcony were two glasses of bourbon, an ash tray holding two cigars, and Karl and Jack rocking in Jack's newly acquired chairs. A light breeze blew in from the coast as they watched the sun tracking into the gulf, ending the day. Jack drew in on his cigar, causing the end to glow in a bright red ember, then released a puff of smoke into the breeze. The men heard the door open on the balcony that neighbored theirs and watched Betty step out, saying, "I'm going to call the kids." Karl held his index finger in the air, indicating he understood.

"You're a lucky man, Karl," Jack said, sipping on his bourbon.

"How do you figure?"

"One woman. Not many can say that," Jack replied.

"Yea, not sure how she put up with me all these years."

"Too bad Gerald couldn't stay around long enough to enjoy this," Jack said.

"He's happier where he is." Karl stared at his cigar.

Jack thought for a moment. "Maybe so," he agreed.

A knock came from his door, and after looking at Karl wondering who could be there, Jack walked through his apartment and pulled open the door. Standing in the doorway were Derrick and Kat, holding hands. "Figured I better come by and make sure you're behaving," Kat grinned.

Jack hugged her before letting them in, saying, "Kiddo, I've been worrying about you."

Derrick and Kat walked in and were greeted by Karl entering the sliding glass doors. "Well, we have some news, and I wanted to tell you guys first," Kat started.

"Hang on, Betty will not want to be left out of news." Karl pushed his way through and disappeared to his apartment.

"Glad to see you guys aren't afraid to hold hands in public," Jack laughed.

Betty rushed in before Karl had time to close their door. "Kat! I'm so happy to see you. Karl said you have good news—are you guys getting married?" she asked excitedly.

Both Derrick and Kat held their hands up. "No, no. Not marriage," Kat laughed.

"Are you pregnant?" Betty asked.

Before Kat could answer, "You better marry her if you are having a child," Karl interrupted.

"No! Not pregnant," Derrick cleared his throat.

"Good grief. Let the kids talk," Jack butted in.

Kat looked at Derrick to start the news. "Cedar Branch was struggling financially and things weren't looking great for the future. Our friend Gerald left the community a large sum of money."

Jack and Karl looked at each other, then back to Derrick. "We know," Jack nonchalantly replied.

"You knew?" Derrick looked at Kat.

"Yea, he told us that Kat talked to him, and he thought either leaving the money or buying Cedar Branch was a good investment," Karl replied.

"Did he tell you that he wanted to build a new fine arts center and hire me as a contracted person to run it?" Kat asked, thinking she would surprise them.

"Yea, he said that way you two could date with no stupid rules in the way," Jack answered.

Kat shook her head. "Is there anything we can surprise you with?" she asked.

"Marriage," Betty smiled, holding her hand.

With a smile, Kat patted the back of her hand. "Let's give that some time."

"Derrick, my good boy, let me pour you a glass and you can join us for a Cuban," Jack put his arm around him.

"Well, I am still working and..."

Betty pulled Kat's arm. "Let me show you a new painting that we hung today." She led Kat toward the door.

Derrick's and Kat's eyes met, and both smiled at each other. "OK, a quick drink. Then Kat and I have to go over plans."

"Jack?" Kat said, stopping at the door. Jack turned to face her, "You will be in my art class!" Kat insisted.

"Depends on the women." He held his glass up to her.

"Violet and her two piece?" Karl laughed.

Standing on Jack's balcony, the three men watched the sun dip into the gulf, causing an explosion of colors that drowned the horizon. "I'm not a touchy feely type guy, but ..." Jack took a breath, "I've had five wives and a countless number of women, always searching for the perfect relationship. I never thought I would have found it with a group of guys in a retirement home."

"Community living!" Karl and Derrick replied simultaneously.

About the Author

Lee DuCote has traveled researching cultures, people, and historical accounts to help create his stories. A native to Louisiana, he writes to give hope and encouragement to others, as well as to entertain and spark the imagination. Lee lives in the Ozark Mountains of Arkansas with his wife and family and is the author of *Fields of Alicia*, *Waterproof*, and *Across Borders*. You can visit him and see more or follow him at the links below:

Connect with Lee DuCote

 www. leeducote. com

 @leeducote

 @leeducote

 www. facebook.com/ authorleeducote

Coming Soon

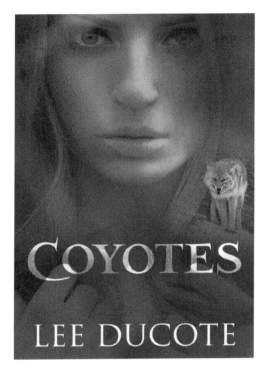

COYOTES

LEE DUCOTE

When Coral La Fleur loses her mother in a mysterious murder at the National Coyote Research Laboratory that also claims the life of three other scientists, her life takes a bizarre and terrifying turn. After visions and dreams of finding herself bonded to a coyote in a way she never imagined possible, Coral seeks help from a young intern, Gavyn Steel, only to find that her visions and dreams are reality. Now they must track down and stop three other rogue coyotes from killing off the residents in a small town tucked away in central Louisiana, all while eluding the military who are tasked with eliminating her and her new furry friend.

Can Coral stop the killing in time and protect her coyote? Will her feelings for Gavyn hinder her efforts?

Find yourself in the footsteps of an animal with the unique ability to adapt to all climates, terrain, and situations in Coral La Fleur's life—except for murder.

Made in the USA
San Bernardino, CA
12 May 2017